"Jonas?" she said, trembling a little

She did not want to shiver like this but she could not control herself.

"Oh, Jonas, is it?" he teased. "Not Brother Wolf? That at least is a little better. Yet somehow, right now, I feel more like Brother Wolf than Jonas Renwick." His wide, lawless blue eyes were riveting Maggie's own, and suddenly she felt she could meet the gaze no longer, yet she still dared not look away. If she did he might advance, and she wanted all her senses, all her saneness, to stop him. Stop him—for Helen's sake.

But in spite of Helen and all that Helen had said, Maggie knew she wanted Jonas Renwick...for herself.

Harlequin Romances
by Joyce Dingwell

These books may be available at your local bookseller.

For a free catalog listing all titles currently available,
send your name and address to:

Harlequin Reader Service
P.O. Box 52040, Phoenix, AZ 85072-9988
Canadian address: Stratford, Ontario N5A 6W2

Brother Wolf

Joyce Dingwell

Harlequin Books

TORONTO • NEW YORK • LONDON
AMSTERDAM • PARIS • SYDNEY • HAMBURG
STOCKHOLM • ATHENS • TOKYO • MILAN

Original hardcover edition published in 1983
by Mills & Boon Limited

ISBN 0-373-02600-5

Harlequin Romance first edition February 1984

Printed in U.S.A.

CHAPTER ONE

THROUGH the aircraft window Maggie watched the first fingers of dawn pushing aside the last shadows of night. It had been barely daylight when the charter had left the town strip, with the result that Maggie had experienced very little of what she had come many miles to see. But now instead of darkness red hills were looking up at her, twisted courses of dried creeks, outcrops of rock, salt pans, clay pans, gibber and desert.

To an Australian easterner, accustomed in Maggie's case to the tropical abundance of the Queensland coast, the raw, bare-boned scene below was a little intimidating. Coming from a world of lush greens and smiling blues the fierce reds and brooding ochres almost dismayed her. And yet, she thought with wonder, the rough escarpments and sandy wastes also oddly attracted her. Even this early in her alien venture she felt herself moving to a new—and stimulating— rhythm.

Maggie had never gone west before, indeed she had never gone anywhere except her own Queensland Barrier Reef, to which beauty spot, as an island hostess, she had sailed weekly to attend to the needs of the coral tourists. Surrounded by trippers of all nationalities, for all the loveliness of her own surroundings stay-at-home Maggie had listened with envy to accounts of other places— America, England, Europe, the world.

'Yet I,' Maggie had complained to her fellow hostess, 'only know white sands and blue lagoons.'

'What better?' had asked Kathy, who had come up from Melbourne one winter and never returned.

'It's all right for you, Kathy,' Maggie had accused, 'you've travelled.'

'But prefer here. Look, Maggie, if you're *really* serious——'

'I'm really serious.'

'Then I'll ask Jonas,' Kathy had said.

'Jonas?' Maggie had enquired.

'Or perhaps Timothy.' Kathy had considered a moment. 'No, not Tim,' she had decided, 'Tim would only smile gently and say "Of course, dear." After which he'd promptly forget. No, Maggie, I'll ask Jonas.'

'What are you talking about, Kathy?' Maggie had begged.

'Jonas and Timothy Renwick are brothers. Also they're here right now—no, not in this boat but on the mainland. They're returning from a business trip north but have loitered long enough at Compass Bay to say hullo.'

'What kind of business? What do they do? Where do they come from?' Maggie had asked curiously, but she had been stopped with a frown and a warning nod to several of the tourists now looking promptingly in the hostesses' direction.

'Morning tea time coming up,' Kathy had reminded her, and the two girls had got busy.

But between their courier services that day and the next day Maggie had learned more from Kathy.

'Phineas Acres is out west, *very west*, and it's

rough, tough, uninviting and altogether quite outrageous. However, if you're still interested——'

'Oh, I am, I am!'

'Then I'll see Jonas,' Kathy had promised.

'Or Timothy,' Maggie had reminded her.

'No, it will definitely be Jonas.'

Maggie had asked Kathy how either Jonas or Timothy Renwick would be interested in *her*.

'In Tim's case because you're pleasant to look at—yes, you are, Maggie—and Tim likes pleasant things.'

'What kind of things?' Maggie had asked warily, and Kathy had laughed.

'Not those kind of things,' she had reassured her friend. 'You're safe. No, Timothy is the family sheep, not at all like Brother Wolf.'

'By Brother Wolf you would mean Jonas?' Maggie had queried.

'Yes, Maggie, but to be fair to him, Jonas isn't that kind of wolf—I mean not a woman wolf, he's more—well——'

'Sharp? Ready to attack?'

'Exactly. Tim is the gentle type, and those pleasant things I spoke of are precious and semi-precious stones. Sapphires, rubies, you name it, and Phineas Acres, or so Tim hopes and dreams, has it.'

'And Brother Wolf,' Maggie had tagged Jonas Renwick, 'what would *his* interest be in me? If not, as you just said, as a woman?'

'Jonas,' Kathy had answered, 'would be interested in what you're doing at this moment, Maggie.'

'Hostessing?'

'Yes. Jonas and Timothy badly need a hostess,

or at least Phineas Acres does. In fact that's what their trip was all about: *Cherchez la femme.* But not *cherchez* for any fancy purposes, strictly for business—hostess business. Why, Jonas even tried to entice me.' Kathy had shrugged. 'Change blue lagoons for dry creeks!' she had derided. 'Not for me.' She had looked at Maggie. 'Possibly for you?'

'Quite possibly, Kathy. I feel I must get out of this pleasant rut. So please tell me more.'

Kathy had complied.

'Cousin Timothy romantically sees Phineas Acres as gem potential,' she had explained, 'but Cousin Jonas materially sees only what he can make from Tim's dream. The financial result, as far as Jonas is concerned, the Phineas Station.'

'A station out there?'

'Yes.'

'Cattle, I suppose.'

'Surprisingly, no. Sheep. Before the present long dry there was quite a prosperous sheep run at Phineas Acres. Fine wool was the goal, and fine wool is what Jones is interested in now.'

'In short, a wolf with sheep inclinations.' Maggie had been unable to resist that. 'How does Brother Wolf plan to prosper from Timothy's gem ambitions?' she had asked.

'The usual way, Maggie. Accommodation for amateur prospectors, caravan parks, the hiring of shovels and buckets, or whatever is needed for prospecting, probably a shop, all the rest of it.'

'All to go to the older brother?'

'Yes.'

'That seems unfair to me.'

'Perhaps, but sheep prospered once, so they could again, according to Jonas, whereas gems are unpredictable, Jonas also says. However, he tolerates them, if only for what might come out of them—for Phineas. You could say sheep are Jonas's babies,' Kathy had grinned.

'I see.' Maggie had been thoughtful a moment. 'Would it be this wolf brother who would hire or fire me?' she had asked Kathy.

'Most certainly Jonas would fire anyone if they didn't suit him.'

'Suit him at what, Kathy?'

'I told you—at what we're doing now. Soothing tourists. And something very different from soothing will be done to us if we don't start a deck game or bingo. Wait until we return from the islands, Maggie, then you can ask the boys yourself.'

'I think you mean one boy, singular.'

Kathy had laughed and moved off.

The 'boys', older than Kathy, and Jonas older than Timothy, had been staying at the Coral hotel at Compass Bay. Maggie had watched Kathy bringing them to the tea garden to meet her, and had sorted them out at once.

That one would be the gem-loving, beauty-minded Timothy, she had judged, he had to be with that dreamy expression, but the other one——

Yes, Kathy had confirmed a moment later, this is Jonas. She had presented Timothy next, and Tim had taken her hand at once, something his brother had not done. Maggie had felt rebuffed, and except that she really wanted to get away from blue lagoons she would have retreated on the spot.

But after they had sat down, Maggie had seen that though she would escape lagoons at Phineas

Acres, she certainly would not escape the colour of blue. Across the small table Jonas Renwick had looked piercingly at Maggie from eyes of brilliant cobalt. Timothy's eyes were russet, Maggie had previously noted, friendly, warm eyes, but Jonas's blue eyes were hard and cool.

'So you would like to leave here?' Jonas Renwick had asked Maggie as he had glanced meaningly to the shining sea between the fronds of the pandanus palms, the distant Barrier Reef islands inset like bright jewels.

Maggie at once had been reminded of Timothy Renwick's hoped-for gems at Phineas Acres, and rather foolishly had included something of the sort in her reply. At once she had been met by a quick narrowing of Jonas Renwick's brilliant blue eyes, a pull to his long mouth.

'*I* am not interested in that angle,' Jonas had said.

'Only in the tourist trade you hope to attract because of it,' Maggie had dared.

'To further my own interest, yes.'

'Sheep.' Sheep are Jonas's babies, Kathy had said.

'I see you've been briefed,' Jonas Renwick had intoned coolly.

'Not really,' Maggie had admitted, 'so, if I'm acceptable, could you please tell me?'

'You have to be acceptable,' he had come back rudely. 'There's nothing else offering.'

'Shouldn't it be no one else offering?' Maggie had suggested.

'I'm sorry.' But Jonas Renwick had said it without sorrow. 'It should have been no one else is keen on anything so rough, tough, uninviting——'

'And altogether outrageous,' Maggie had tacked on, using Kathy's description.

'No need for me to go on,' he had shrugged, 'for you've certainly been warned. How soon, Miss Wentworth, could you report to Rakatoo?'

'Rakatoo?' she queried.

'Our nearest town with an accommodating airstrip. You could fly direct to there from here, from Compass Bay to Rakatoo. After that we would charter you out to as near as possible to Phineas Acres.'

'Not right out?' For some reason Maggie chose to be perverse.

'No, that's only possible for a small craft like——' But for some reason Jonas Renwick had not continued.

Maggie had waited a moment, then mused aloud: 'Sheep and precious stones.'

'Very few sheep right now,' Jonas Renwick had regretted, 'years of too much dry have seen to that. But the dry, it appears, have seen to stones, or so my brother tells me, and the stones to a tourist influx ... or so we hope. For that reason I've had built a motel, a camping area, a depot for the hiring of gear, the rest of the stint, but what I have not done, but must, I'm told, is provide for the female side. No' ... at a quick look from Maggie ... 'not domestic chores, the male staff will see to that, but—well, a woman around the house. Houses, actually.' He had smiled perfunctorily, but, as far as Maggie was concerned, his smile was not a success. Did his cobalt-blue eyes have to glitter quite like that? Did his long mouth have to pull so sarcastically to one side?

'There is also,' he had drawled, 'a small store.'

'My responsibility?' Maggie had asked.

'If you accept this job, yes.' He had mentioned a remuneration figure.

'I accept.' Maggie had heard her own voice committing her to serve this entirely unattractive, even hostile person, and she had wondered how she could be so foolish. It wasn't as though she needed to leave home, leave the firm, she could stop on with the coral service for as long as she liked, and blue lagoons certainly were much nicer than dry creeks.

However, she had still assented, probably because of Timothy Renwick's reassuring look, and within the hour the brothers had flown out.

A week later Maggie had done the same thing, and now ... in minutes, the pilot was telling Maggie ... they would be landing at Phineas Acres, or as near to P.A. as they could. There was no strip at Phineas, the pilot added, only a smallish paddock where the de Merril girl landed in her Cessna. The pilot gave Maggie a meaningful look at his, but without her encouragement he left it at that.

No doubt, he added, one of the Renwick boys will have come out to fetch you.

I only hope, Maggie thought, that 'boy' is Tim.

It was Tim. The gem brother climbed out of a four-wheel-drive and came eagerly over to Maggie, his hand extended.

While the charter pilot brought out her bags, Maggie said impulsively: 'I'm glad it's you.'

Tim smiled and answered: 'I'm glad you're

glad.' He added, loyal to his brother, no doubt: 'Why?'

Why, thought Maggie, with the other alternative? Aloud she said: 'Because you can point out rocks to me.'

'Yes, I'm afraid I will.' Tim Renwick said goodbye to the pilot, and when the charter plane was in the sky he turned again to Maggie.

'My brother Jonas warns me about being a bore, so I'll try not to be. I'll stow your belongings and we'll push off.'

In minutes they were leaving the bush strip.

Although the going was rough, tough, uninviting and altogether outrageous, as Kathy had told her, Maggie also found it intriguing. At once she was delighted with the names that rolled off Tim's tongue: Silent Gorge, Painted Mountain, Skeleton Corner, Dead Man's Gap.

Tim stopped the waggon to show Maggie some quartzite formation. She found it so interesting that she dared ask him about his other fascination.

'You mean my precious, or semi-precious, hopes?' he interpreted. 'Yes, I've had several evidences of them. Small instances so far, but at the end of the rainbow——'

'Will be a pot of diamonds,' Maggie wished for him.

Tim began driving again, saying as he did: 'You're very encouraging to talk to, Miss Wentworth. My brother Jonas is not.'

'Yet you do what he wants,' Maggie said as tactfully as she could.

'Jonas is the leader—he always was. Anyway, he's bound to be right.'

'But is he right about sheep?' Maggie asked

dubiously, for now they were driving over a
stretch of featureless ochre dust.

'This land was good once,' Tim said. 'I can't
remember it, but I've always been told. Jonas says
it will come good again.'

'For sheep, no doubt.'

'He hopes so.'

'And you don't mind your brother using you
like this? I really mean you don't mind any finds
you make furthering his own interest?'

'I only mind harmonious things,' Tim said
simply. 'Rock is harmonious. I remember my first
find, a small singing emerald.' Quite unexpectedly
he turned to a surprised Maggie. 'You are
harmonious, Miss Wentworth.'

To say the least Maggie was startled. As an
island hostess she had grown accustomed to many
compliments, but never one like this. All she could
blurt out was: 'But I'm yellow, Mr Renwick.'

'Harmonious,' Tim Renwick repeated. 'Also I
call that paleness silver.'

'The wrong colour, anyhow, for out west,'
Maggie mourned, for already her hair was
powdered with red dust.

'So was my emerald, if you come to that.
Singing green against drab!—Miss Wentworth, can
I call you Margaret? That is your name, I think.'

'I get called Maggie. Can I call you Tim?'

'Done,' he smiled. 'We're nearly there—only
over the next hill.'

'Hill?' Maggie laughed at the flatness.

'We call it that here,' Tim assured her. 'You
will, too. Over the next hill, Maggie, is our Reptile
River,' he went on. 'Except that it's not a river any
more, it's quite dry, has been for years. But it

wasn't once. There was quite a parcel of water. There's a disused mine near it, so evidently I wasn't the first rock Renwick; one of my ancestors must have tinkered around, too. The water no doubt was very useful for the mining activity as well as for the sheep. When the stream dried up the sheep naturally had to be reduced, but the mine, of course, withered.'

'Nothing doing there since, Tim?' Maggie asked.

'It would be unsafe, and anyway, amateur prospectors prefer to try their luck on top, never below. They use geological picks and crash hammers, not drills. They avoid the mine. I do myself.' For a brief moment Tim turned his russet eyes on Maggie. 'You must never go either,' he told her. A pause. 'I mean that.'

'You sound serious,' Maggie observed.

'I am serious,' he concurred.

'Then thank you for telling me,' Maggie nodded. 'I wonder, will you tell me something else?'

'Of course.'

'Tell me why I was brought here for a woman's touch when there's a woman already,' she said.

'There's not,' Tim returned.

'The de Merril girl.' Maggie waited. She waited a long time, but was still met with silence. She moistened her lips to try again, then grew silent herself.

The waggon chunted on, and there was a hill after all, for there were grunts and gasps from the engine before the incline was conquered. Maggie looked eagerly over the other side and saw Phineas Acres spread out like a jigsaw puzzle, the dried up river, the rock outcrops, the waste, the derelict mine ... For some reason her eyes rested on the mine ... Then, set incongruously in it all, incongruous since the busyness was too unexpected, too urban, a motel, a store, a hall, a park, a bunkhouse, a canteen——

And a boss.

For the boss of the new Renwick project was undoubtedly Jonas Renwick.

He was putting a nail into one of the walls of the yet incomplete motel, and very deliberately he took his time finishing the task before he replaced the hammer and stepped down from the verandah.

But not to greet Maggie, Maggie soon found, for his first words were to his brother, and they were an order.

'Take her bags over to the homestead, she'll be bunking there.' 'She', noted Maggie, and she stiffened.

Only after Tim, unaided, had removed the bags and carried them off did Jonas Renwick turn to look at Maggie. A long look, cool, rather uninterested.

'Welcome, etcetera, etcetera,' he said with definite _un_welcome.

His cobalt eyes told Maggie it was her turn.

CHAPTER TWO

'How do you do, Mr Renwick,' Maggie said with an equal lack of enthusiasm. 'Do I follow your brother and my bags?'

'Presently, Miss Wentworth. Immediately I have

a few words to say to you. Shall I say them in my office?'

'Is there an office as well!' Maggie asked in mock awe.

He did not bother to answer her. He said shortly: 'Follow me, please,' and started off. He had very long legs, and he did not allow for Maggie's shorter steps, so she had to hurry to keep up with him. She was hot by the time she reached the small detached building which evidently was the office. She was not used to the dry western weather, and knew she must look wilted, sticky, and altogether unattractive. Wet tow hair always changed her into a pathetic waif.

'Take the weight off your feet,' he tossed at her, and Maggie found herself a chair. It was placed away from his desk, but if he had not the manners to draw the chair up, then she was not going to do it for him. He would simply have to speak louder. She sat down.

Jonas Renwick did not speak louder. He had a low-pitched voice and he did not alter it for his visitor. But because he spoke the characteristic slow western drawl, Maggie could hear every word. Nonetheless she wickedly pulled him up several times to ask him to repeat what he had said. At last in irritation he got up from his chair and sat on the edge of the desk nearest to her, his long corduroy legs not far from hers.

'I've housed you in the old homestead, Miss Wentworth,' he told her.

'Bunked, not housed, was the original word,' Maggie corrected him.

He ignored that. 'You might not have noticed the Renwick homestead among the new buildings, but I assure you it's there. You will be living with Grandfather.'

'Grandfather?' Now Maggie looked up.

'Yes, Grandfather is still with us. No doubt' . . . a thin smile . . . 'he'll love you on sight.' Jonas was now estimating Maggie. It was a long, level, cool stare, and Maggie felt embarrassed.

'You mean I'm the type to attract grandfathers,' she interpreted.

'Exactly,' he came back. 'Indeed, the majority of males.'

Maggie, though she felt like inserting that Jonas Renwick undeniably would be in the minority, instead sat on and waited. She felt there was more to come.

'I noted my brother's dreamy look when you arrived just now,' Jonas continued. 'I don't know how susceptible you are, Miss Wentworth, but were I you I would put no weight on it.'

'On what?'

'Dreamy looks.'

'Also what do you infer by "weight"?'

'I think you followed me,' Jonas said drily.

'Yes, I think I did. If it was what I believe you were suggesting, then I must tell you right now that I certainly didn't come west with any—well—design.'

'Go west, young man, but never west, young woman?' Jonas Renwick gave an incredulous laugh. 'What rot! Of course you came with a design, whether you were actually aware of it or not. All women have design. I think a view to marriage is the first lesson they're taught as babies. Then remember Eve. That's why I'm warning you now. Discard any thoughts you might have of

Timothy. Tim has merely looked upon you and admired in you—well, whatever he's currently admiring. What is it? Did he say?'

'Diamonds, rubies, emeralds,' Maggie said recklessly. This man, this quite impossible man! she thought.

'Three of the best!' Jonas whistled. 'Tim must have been really smitten.'

'He wasn't speaking of me.' Maggie's voice was tight.

'But his senses were,' Jonas insinuated. 'Timothy is extremely aware of pretty things.'

'I'm not pretty,' Maggie shrugged.

'I entirely agree. But it's all, remember, in the eye of the beholder, and I have a fair idea of how my brother beholds.'

Wondering how this man would react if she mentioned Tim's word 'harmonious', Maggie rushed in with: 'Can we leave this subject, please?'

'Only after I add that there would be no use, either, having designs on me.' Jonas smiled blandly.

'You—why, you——'

'Again I entirely agree,' Jonas drawled. 'That warning was uncalled for, quite unnecessary, but it still had to be said. Ideas always should be talked out, in case, in some unclear fashion, they become established facts. Being alerted saves a deal of trouble later.'

'The trouble in this instance being the ridiculous possibility of you and me,' Maggie fumed.

'If it salves your wounded ego, Miss Wentworth, I and any woman. It's not particularly you.'

'In other words, you don't care for the female sex, Mr Renwick?'

'I think we'd better get on first name terms. Call me Jonas. Out here it would sound absurd saying Mister.'

'If I can help it I won't be calling you anything,' Maggie assured him. 'But thank you for my answer. You don't like women.'

'An understatement,' he agreed levelly. He waited for that to sink in.

'Now that we know each other,' he said, 'I shall tell you about Grandfather. You looked surprised just now when I said Grandfather—do I appear too old to you to have a grandfather? Do I even look one myself?'

'Perish *that* thought!' The words were out before Maggie could stop them.

'Yes, perish it,' he agreed wholeheartedly. 'To be a grandfather would require progeny from me to ensure more progeny, and that entails female help.'

'Help?' Maggie looked incredulously at Jonas. What sort of man *was* this?

'Well, co-operation,' he allowed, 'certainly a second sex.'

Maggie fumed silently for a few moments, then she said: 'I know now why your cousin Kathy named you the wolf brother, though not necessarily the woman-wolf variety. You're certainly not that.'

'You sound a little bitter,' he commented mildly. 'could it be you would have preferred it the other way round?'

'Certainly not!' Maggie felt her cheeks burning. Never, she said under her breath, from you. A quick glance at Jonas startled her, it was almost as though she had spoken her thoughts aloud. She saw the glitter of his eyes, the twist to his mouth again.

'So we understand each other,' Jonas drawled, 'which is a wise thing. However, best not to be too positive. The winds of change are always with us, aren't they?' One of his eyebrows lifted sardonically.

'There'll be no wind of change with me,' Maggie promised.

He did not promise the same himself, and inexplicably uneasy, and hating herself for it, Maggie prompted: 'You were speaking of your grandfather.'

'Yes, I'm putting you in the old house with him.' A pause. 'No, bunking you there, as you rightly corrected. Reason being that although one does not expect wolf-men among rock-men it's always better to be wise before the act.'

'Act?'

Jonas grinned and shrugged.

'I also,' he admitted frankly, 'need your motel space.'

'Of course. Thank you for the honesty.' Maggie's voice was thin. 'But aren't you being rather optimistic expecting to fill a new project, a new venture, so soon?'

'On the contrary, we're completely booked out, the caravan park filled already, the motel expecting to be. Australia has gone gem-crazy. Everyone seems to have the belief that if you dig a hole out here you find something.'

'You don't have that idea?' Maggie asked him.

'I don't even give it a thought, except for what it can bring me.'

'More sheep?'

'Better sheep. I'm going in for a special breed. The gems, if they do exist, can help me, but if they don't, then the fools looking for them can.'

'You mean Tim's "fools" can help you?' Maggie asked with scorn.

'Yes.' After a moment he challenged: 'Why not?'

'Alternatively—why?' Maggie dared.

He looked at her in pretended puzzlement.

'Why does it have to be help *to you*?' Maggie flashed.

'For me and not my brother?' Jonas interpreted. 'It's because I deal with living things, not dreams.'

'Yet Tim indicated to me that he's not dealing just with dreams,' Maggie defended, 'he says he has had several instances.'

'I don't care if he has had coffers of instances, it would still be coffers of inert things. I work with flesh and blood.'

'Sheep variety,' stated Maggie.

He looked at her narrowly. 'Do you think I should deal in any other variety of flesh and blood?' His cobalt eyes glittered at her.

'I think,' said Maggie, 'I could do with a shower.'

'You shall have one,' he promised. 'Your digs are over in the homestead, as I told you. Right there.' He pointed through the office window to something Maggie had not noticed before: an old house. It was the traditional pioneer home of four generations ago, generous, weatherworn, surrounded entirely by wide verandahs.

'Do I drive you?' Jonas asked lazily.

'Of course not,' Maggie snapped, for it was only some hundred yards. 'Will your grandfather be there?'

'Where else?' Jonas Renwick shrugged at the

emptiness beyond all the busyness he had created. 'Yes, Grandfather will be waiting for you. You're an event. Meet him, take your shower, settle in, then come back and we'll go on from where we left off.'

Resisting an impulse to ask where that was, Maggie nodded casually, and left.

She began crossing to the old homestead, secretly marvelling as she did at the number of things Jonas Renwick had done, at what the fellow had achieved. He had taken a western waste and transformed it into a tourist city. Also he had done it punctually as well as efficiently, Maggie sensed, for it had been clear to her when Jonas had replaced his hammer as she had arrived that he had been driving home a final nail. There had been unmistakable self-satisfaction in the act, knowledge of a job well done. This man would always be satisfied with himself, she thought, always finish what he began. Impatient with her observations, Maggie looked around.

The motel was not occupied yet, but the caravan park was. Probably by tomorrow the entire project would be buzzing—booked out, Jonas Renwick had said. Everyone gem-crazy. Why not, Maggie allowed, it all sounded fun . . . and for one man it promised much more than fun, it assured reward. Good for Brother Wolf, Maggie grimaced, but not so good for Tim. Poor Tim.

She reached the big square homestead with the customary large front door wide open and displaying the usual long hallway with rooms on each side. At the top of a shallow flight of steps stood an old man. His hand was outstretched and he was smiling at her.

'I know all about you—well' . . . another smile
. . . 'I know your name. Come in, girl.'

'Hullo, Grandfather,' Maggie smiled back. She
took his hand and tried to return the firm grasp.

'Hullo, Maggie.' He nodded to her to follow
him down the hall to the kitchen, where Maggie
already knew tea would be waiting on a capacious
table, chairs drawn up, a large brown pot letting
off steam, cups laid out.

On either side of the hallway were the expected
ranks of bedrooms.

'Take your pick,' Grandfather invited.

It seemed that a decision had already been made
for her, for in one of the rooms her bags had been
placed beside a bed.

'This one will do, Grandfather,' she nodded, still
following the old man to the kitchen.

Just as she had known, everything awaited. The
amber brew was ready to pour, milk was
produced, sugar, a large cake.

'Well now,' beamed Grandfather when he had
finished serving Maggie, but continued looking
admiringly at her, 'I don't think they'll like this at
all, I think they'll be annoyed.'

'They?' inquired Maggie.

'The de Merrils.'—The de Merril girl, Maggie
recalled from the charter pilot.

'Who are?' she asked Grandfather.

'Our next-door neighbours.'

Maggie looked outside the kitchen window to
the ochre endlessness beyond Jonas's tourist
scheme.

'How far is next-door, Grandfather?' she asked.

'Oh, close, Maggie. No more than a hundred
miles.'

'A hundred——?' Maggie smiled. 'Then they won't be liking or not liking it, will they? Not from a hundred miles.'

'With Helen here every day,' stated Grandfather.

'Helen?'

'Helen de Merril, the granddaughter.'

'Surely she isn't here that often?' Maggie accepted more cake. 'Not from a hundred miles.'

'She flies her own plane, Maggie. Right from a little girl she was mechanically-minded. She even flew his.'

'His?'

'Her father's.' Grandfather cut some cake for himself. 'Now it's hers, and she flies it here.'

'I see.' Maggie was recalling Jonas's unfinished reply to her that only a small craft could land at Phineas. Adding that to the charter pilot's few meaning words she knew the small craft must be Helen de Merril's.

'Not every day?' she doubted.

'Yes,' Grandfather insisted.

'She works here, then?' Jonas Renwick had said he needed a woman around the house, so perhaps there *were* two of them, in spite of Tim's denial.

'Oh, no, Helen doesn't work here.' Grandfather shook his head very definitely. 'Oh, no,' he said again.

Something in his voice alerted Maggie, and she looked enquiringly at him. He caught the look, but returned nothing.

'If that room will do you,' he proposed, 'I'll help you unpack at once. Yes' . . . at Maggie's smile . . . 'I used to do it for Linda. She was my daughter-in-law, my son William's wife. The boys' mother.' His voice faltered and Maggie noticed it.

'Was, Grandfather?' she asked gently.

'She's gone now.'

'Gone?'

'There was this disaster . . . this accident. It was a road accident, on the way up here.'

'To Phineas?'

'To the de Merril place as well. The two families were travelling back together.'

'Was it only Linda who——' Maggie's voice trailed off.

'No, Maggie. The four of them—Linda, my son William, Teresa and Maxim de Merril.'

'That's terrible,' Maggie said sadly.

'The young ones were in the car, too.'

'You mean Jonas and Timothy?'

'And the daughter of the other couple—Helen.'

'Helen who now flies across.'

'Yes. Helen de Merril. The three children escaped.' A long pause. 'It's years ago now, water under the bridge. I took over the boys, of course. Her own grandparents came here and took over Helen. If you've finished, Maggie, I'll settle you in.'

As obviously Grandfather wished to help her, and at the same time change the subject, Maggie got up from the table. When she reached the allotted room she saw why Grandfather was so eager. He wanted to see her reaction, and Maggie's reaction was pure bliss.

It was a turn-of-the-century bedroom that met her enchanted gaze, not a minute younger, an old brass bed covered with a marcella quilt, a china washbasin with sprigged roses, a rag mat.

'I see you like it, Maggie.' Grandfather was well

pleased. 'You can't always tell. Linda never did. She called it antiquated. But then neither she nor my son cared at all for Phineas. They only tolerated it between their escapes to civilisation. Civilisation is what they called everywhere else but home. It was coming back from one of those visits that——' The old man stopped, and looked away.

Maggie put her hand gently on his, and presently he turned back to her and smiled.

'A lot of water,' he said again. 'My own son preferred the crowds, but his son only wants Phineas, just as I always wanted it. A skipped generation, would you say?' He looked quizzically at Maggie, deep pride there as well.

Maggie answered him with a question. 'Jonas or Timothy?' she asked.

'Timothy?' Grandfather said in surprise. He said only that, but for Maggie it was more than enough. A minute went by.

Resentful for Tim, but reminding herself that she was an outsider, Maggie changed the subject by asking practically if the remainder of the homestead was last century.

'Bathroom and kitchen modernised on Jonas's insistence, but all the other rooms are the same as when I first brought my dear wife here.'

'Have you been alone long, Grandfather?' she asked gently.

'Too long,' the old man sighed. 'Yet I wouldn't have had it the other way.'

'I think you're telling me that your wife died before the accident, so was spared the pain,' Maggie interpreted.

'Yes,' nodded Grandfather gratefully. 'You're a

perceptive girl.' He said once more: 'They'll be annoyed.'

'The de Merrils?'

'Yes.'

'At my being perceptive,' Maggie smiled.

'At you being here at all, especially at the same time as Helen. Helen has never had anyone else around, and although everything was taking a long, long time, I know they were still waiting for it to happen.'

'The de Merrils?' Maggie asked again.

'Yes,' Grandfather told her again.

'Waiting for what to happen?'

Grandfather looked levelly at Maggie. 'For their granddaughter to be Helen Renwick, not Helen de Merril,' he said. 'But now' . . . he spread his old hands and smiled at her, 'Maggie has come.'

CHAPTER THREE

MAGGIE has come to what?

Maggie was asking herself this as she came down the homestead's long cool hall. She was going to take a walk.

Grandfather had pleaded his age as an excuse for retiring for his afternoon nap, and it had seemed a good time to Maggie to explore.

What have I come to? she thought whimsically, looking ahead of her to the glare and heat of the sun. I don't know yet, she decided, but I do know there are a few mysteries.

Mystery One: The de Merrils won't like this at all, meaning, I interpret, the de Merrils won't like me. Why won't they like me?

Mystery Two: The de Merrils are waiting for a Helen Renwick, not a Helen de Merril. Well, judged Maggie of that, all I can say is: 'Poor Helen!'

She meant poor Helen. Tim, for all his innate niceness, would be an elusive prize, she judged; dreamers like Tim inevitably were. As for Jonas Renwick, had he not readily agreed that he hated women? This left Helen at a distinct disadvantage, so where, and Maggie descended the verandah steps, could her arrival here make it any worse?

If it was only marriage, and not marriage exclusively with a Renwick, that was desired by the de Merrils, there should be more candidates now that the project was functioning. But Grandfather had said Helen *Renwick*, and that restricted things. Why did it have to be a Renwick for this Helen? Why did it have to be anyone in these changed times? Why did Helen de Merril fly over here every day? Why many things, Maggie thought.

There were other mysteries as well as the de Merrils, there were the Renwicks. Timothy Renwick's nice but strained, abstracted air, Jonas Renwick's far from nice animosity against an employee he himself had accepted.

Even the names out here were strange: Silent Gorge, Painted Mountain, Skeleton Corner, Dead Man's Gap.

Maggie, impatient with mysteries, looked around her and decided on a brief walk to clear her muddled brain as well as get a general idea of the place.

The first thing that struck her, apart from the

glittering sun, was the care Jonas Renwick had taken with his scheme. She had expected the usual pre-fab buildings, the usual pre-fab finish. But Brother Wolf ... she found herself calling him that absurd name ... either by luck, or art had given every one of his constructions a charming touch. The motel section had a rustic presentation, the store had been built on old trading post lines, and above the entrance to the caravan park and camping area were totem poles, no doubt symbols of welcome.

Maggie made first of all for the motel, which she knew was not yet occupied, if soon to be. As she walked across she noticed a door of the row of units slightly ajar, and decided to have a peep. She climbed a small flight of shallow stairs, crossed the verandah, the slid herself within.

She had advanced a few steps before she realised that the unit was in use after all, and at once was annoyed with her careless intrusion. She should have looked closer before she went in, she should have checked that no car indicating a guest stood outside. But, checking now, no car stood there, so how had the occupant arrived?

'I flew.' The two words came across the small but tasteful suite. Maggie, whipping her glance from the golden glare to the subdued tones of the interior, took a few moments to focus the speaker. Then she saw a girl, her own age, perhaps a little older, and very pretty.

'I think you must be Helen,' Maggie said pleasantly, but the pleasantness did not help her.

'Yes,' the girl said, and left it at that.

A silence fell between them, a quiet that Maggie felt she must break before it became established.

'The curtains are pretty,' she admired. 'Did you do them?'

'No.'

'I really meant did you scheme them?'

'No.'

'They match this country—gold, red, ochre.' A pause. 'I come from the coast.'

No comment.

'My name' . . . a little desperately . . . 'is Maggie Wentworth. I've come to Phineas Acres to——' But Maggie could hardly say to be a woman around the house, not to another woman. She told Helen instead: 'To mind the store.'

'Yes,' Helen de Merril said.

'You fly.'

'Yes.'

'That's clever.'

'No. Many western women fly.'

'All the same I'm sure I could never do it.'

The girl said nothing. While Maggie was searching for something else to break the silence, Helen de Merril went silently out of the motel, not even nodding to Maggie as she left.

After a confused few minutes Maggie went as far as the verandah, where she stood in complete puzzlement. What had she said? Or not said?

Within moments she heard the whirr of an engine, and looking skywards she saw a small plane ascending. The paddock, she concluded, must be quite near. She watched until the aircraft was out of sight, then, shrugging, decided on a further tour of discovery.

The store was not open, so Maggie was unable to examine the goods she would be expected to sell, but at least she ascertained when she would be

selling them. A notice on the door announced that
trading was one hour in the morning and one hour
in the evening, commencing today. Maggie was
appalled. It was preposterous expecting her to
start so soon after a long journey, but—she hoped
—whoever had attended the shop earlier would do
so, on her behalf, again tonight. For this reason
she ignored the opening hours, and instead
scanned a second notice. It was headed Rock
Tours, and she read that they were available every
afternoon at a given price. Jonas Renwick
certainly was letting no opportunity slip out of his
greedy grasp, she thought. How many tours, she
wondered coldly, would buy a hungry wolf a
sheep?

She turned from the store and looked embrac-
ingly around her. What a completely incongruous,
yet fascinating, place it was. She found herself
eager to explore every corner, particularly, in spite
of Tim's solemn warning, the old, disused mine.
As earlier today she stared intently at the derelict
erection. It seemed to beckon her, even compel
her, and except that it was too late now to start
off, she would have walked over at once. Tim, she
thought fondly, for somehow one had to think
fondly of Tim, need never know.

But instead, looking at her watch, Maggie began
walking back to the homestead, taking a different
route from the one she had taken when she had
left. She had not gone far when she noticed a
carefully enclosed paddock adjacent to the old
house, such a pampered corral she was sure at
once it must be for no other purpose than Brother
Wolf's 'babies'. For his precious sheep.

She strolled curiously across and looked in. The

sheep must be very precious, she decided, for they numbered no more than an exclusive thirty.

'But each worth a small fortune.' In her absorption Maggie had not heard Jonas Renwick's steps behind her. 'They're stud stuff—top drawer.'

'Apparently.' Maggie nodded to the meticulous fencing, no fear of any damage to the occupants in this pampered pen.

Jonas had hoisted himself on to the fence, and was holding out a hand to Maggie to do likewise. She shook her head. He did not comment. He reached in his pocket and took out a pipe.

'You don't sound over-impressed,' he observed. 'Doubtless you're impressed elsewhere. Doubtless you're gem-struck, like my brother is, like the rest of them are here.'

'I wouldn't say so,' Maggie returned, 'but I would admit there's a certain thrill in rock. Something' ... she searched for a word, then announced it triumphantly, 'natal.'

'What?' In the middle of preparing the pipe he changed his mind, and returned it to his pocket.

'Natal,' Maggie repeated.

'Meaning?'

'A beginning.' Again Maggie was triumphant. She said: 'Wouldn't rock be that? The beginning of everything?'

Jonas did not agree. 'To Tim's mind, and yours, it might be, but never to mine. Natal to me means birth, and birth deals in life.'

'In flesh and blood, you're going to say next,' observed Maggie.

'Yes.'

'Sheep variety?' She had said that before.

'Do you think I should deal in any other

variety?' He had answered that before, and his cobalt eyes had glittered at her as they were glittering now.

Maggie did not reply.

'I could never get stirred up over something that does not live,' Jonas announced. 'I prefer what's on our earth, not in it. What's around me.' He began looking around him, but abruptly halted his gaze at Maggie, and she was suddenly aware of a protesting quiver somewhere within her, an unwanted awareness of him, almost an expectancy.

She turned away from the fence.

She went a few steps before she turned back again. In all honesty she knew she should tell him that she, too, liked living things, that she had never been a lover of the fossils of yesterday compared to the breathing reality of today. She heard herself murmuring: 'I like those, too,' to the man who had now descended from the fence and come to stand beside her.

'Those?' Jonas asked. His eyes were narrowed.

'What you just said,' Maggie mumbled uncomfortably, wondering what he would answer to that.

He answered at once—witheringly. He said: 'No need to suck up to the boss.'

'I did no such thing!' she protested.

'Then it sounded damn like it.' He looked directly at her. 'It would do you no good, you know.'

'Do I need good done to me?' Maggie demanded furiously.

'I don't know,' he came back. 'Do you? All I do know is I could make it worse for you. Or' ... provocatively ... 'would it be worse?'

'What would be worse? What are you talking about?'

'Would it be worse if I lived up to that name you've tagged me, Miss Wentworth? Would it be a punishment—or a reward?'

'What name?' evaded Maggie.

'Oh, come off it, you know what I mean.'

'Brother Wolf,' Maggie nodded. 'It would, of course, be worse. But aren't you forgetting something?' He raised his brows at her. 'Aren't you forgetting you're a woman-hater?' Maggie asked.

'Well?' he encouraged.

'Aren't you forgetting that wolves and woman-haters are poles apart?'

'Not all those poles,' he suggested laconically. 'Even a woman-hater can do what a man can do, and he sometimes does. Oh, yes, Miss Wentworth, he can "make love" . . . surely the most ridiculous two words in the world . . . with the same result.' He actually grinned, but Maggie burned.

'You mean you would actually take a woman——' she blurted, then stopped.

'Because I had a need? Yes.'

'Then you are indeed Brother Wolf.' Maggie began to walk away.

Before she could go far he shot out a quick hand and detained her. She started to pull . . . then stopped. It was not his hold that prevented her, for that was light, almost inconsequential, it was the touch of him. It was so male, so vital, so intentional that she suddenly felt compelled by it, even mastered, enslaved. In some unconscious way she must have communicated how she felt to him, for he took away his hand and instead tilted her chin.

'Don't be frightened, Maggie,' he intoned in a low voice, 'I'm no wolf, you can see I haven't the right-coloured eyes.'

'Blue,' Maggie murmured unclearly, very aware of his closeness.

'You've noticed!' He grinned at her. He let her go. 'You'd better get back to the homestead if you're to open the store on time tonight—oh, yes, I know you know about it, I saw you reading my notice.'

Was there nothing he did not see? Irritated, Maggie complained: 'There'll be no customers to open up for.'

'There will be many,' he corrected her. 'The reason you haven't seen anyone around is because my—Tim's—people are all out fossicking, not merely filling in their idle hours in sun-worship or shops.'

'My people studied the coral,' Maggie informed coldly. 'Anyway, what difference could it make?'

'The difference of available time,' he pointed out. 'Your tourists had all day to squander, these have only a session morning and night—the difference, you could say, of serious application to lying golden and naked on the sand.'

Because his eyes were raking her, Maggie shot: 'I was a hostess, not a tourist.'

'Then golden,' he amended, but his eyes never left her, and Maggie felt the other as well.

'I think,' she heard him saying, 'you'd better go after all. You might not be pretty, as you and I agreed earlier, but you do have a certain—well——' He stopped to grin. It made him actually that wolf, Maggie thought. She wasted no time, she wheeled around and ran.

As she did so she was infuriated to hear him deliberately making howling sounds from behind her, and she glanced back to find him matching her furious pace with his more leisurely steps, for he had the advantage of those longer legs. But at least he was not howling devilishly any more, he was laughing openly at her disgust.

'From eight o'clock to nine o'clock,' he shouted at her. 'Same hour in the morning!'

Maggie ignored him and kept running to the house.

Grandfather had the meal ready. It was simple but perfectly presented, and the old man accepted Maggie's praise with pleasure.

'I've done my share of cooking,' he told her. 'I had to, after Mary died. Then when I inherited Jonas and Timothy the domestic chores took over from the station.'

'You've done very well, Grandfather,' Maggie said. Under her breath she added that Grandfather had done well *with Tim*.

Grandfather had propped his elbows on the table and his chin on his palms. He looked thoughtful.

'Jonas is doing miracles with his sheep,' he mused, 'and if the old river ever comes good again Phineas Acres will be right on top. Yes, I've done well with Jonas, but the other one——'

'Tim,' Maggie said carefully.

'Yes, Tim. I don't know Tim at all. I never did,' he sighed.

Maggie tried to help by remarking that it had been a lot to ask of him.

'There was no one else to be asked, on both sides.'

'Both sides, Grandfather?' she queried.

'Helen's, as well. It was much harder for the de Merrils. You see, they had to leave their own home. I just stayed on here.'

'Did they come far?' Maggie asked.

'Europe.'

'Europe?' Maggie was surprised.

'Jonas could tell you where.' Suddenly Grandfather looked very tired. 'Imagine two old people, for they are older than I am, Maggie, leaving over there for here.' He looked beyond the kitchen window to the ochre endlessness.

'Couldn't Helen have gone to them?' Maggie suggested.

'Not according to the de Merrils. They were rigid people, traditional. They had rules. Their only child, Helen's father Maxim, must have disappointed them badly when he chose, after a visit here, to remain in Australia, become Australian, but they still respected and accepted what their son had done. They considered Maxim the head of his house here even after his death, and they never questioned that his child Helen could be anything but Australian in her turn. It was a way they looked at things, and they never faltered. *They* came *here*.' Grandfather lapsed into a long silence.

Maggie broke it.

'I met Helen,' she said quietly.

'I see.' Grandfather looked across the table at Maggie.

'Do you see?' Maggie asked. 'Is she like that with you as well?'

'She never comes up here,' Grandfather said. Before Maggie could go on he told her: 'There's apple pie—I thought you might like that. Do you mind cream out of a can?'

The topic was closed.

Around eight Maggie crossed reluctantly to the store. It was all quite ridiculous, she still believed; there would be nobody to serve.

But scarcely had she left the homestead than she noted the flickering camp and caravan lights. The motel might not be opened yet, but the more al-fresco section of the guests were well represented, and by the crowd gathered around the shop when she reached it many were needing her services.

Jonas Renwick had already opened up for her, and would, he told Maggie, stay on to assist her. *Tonight.*

'After that,' he said, 'I'll send Tim, make him earn some of his keep.'

'Surely he has enough on his plate,' Maggie retorted. 'I read on your notice board that there were rock tours. Presumably he would be the conductor.'

'Only,' Jonas gritted, 'when he conducts. We only started today, but he's already forgotten. Look, Miss Wentworth, the edible section is at this end, the toilet goods and medicine at that, the reading matter in between. You'll catch on as you get asked for things, and what you can't find the customer will find for himself.'

'Hopefully,' Maggie shrugged.

'No, positively—I had a trial run last night. Stand back for the rush.'

The customers proved a genial lot, tending to stand round in groups as they discussed their day's prospecting, forgetting what they had come for and having to be prompted. Most of them purchased more equipment. All, Maggie decided, bought paperbacks.

'No television,' Jonas expained slyly, 'nothing to do but go to bed. And since the majority of them have left their wives behind, naturally the books are booming.' He smiled evilly at Maggie's distaste. 'What else did you expect from a wolf?'

'Nothing,' Maggie assured him. She saw that he was looking at the wall clock.

'Time, gentlemen!' he called humorously, and there was a last-minute spate of buying, then the door was closed.

Jonas Renwick wasted no time in dismissing Maggie.

'You can go, too. Tidy up tomorrow.' He looked at her speculatively. 'You must be tired.'

It was the first consideration he had given her, and Maggie looked at him in surprise.

'I'm a bit that way myself,' he shrugged. 'Goodnight, Miss Wentworth. Take this.' He placed something in her hand, and, looking down, Maggie saw it was a torch.

'No street lights here,' he reminded her. 'You'll need it.' Evidently he needed nothing himself, for in moments he had left.

But in spite of the sudden dark Maggie did not switch on the torch at once. *Not* so much the wolf, she was thinking irresistibly, not—looking upward—for such a night as this. She had not known that western nights would be so breathlessly beautiful—navy blue sky, a golden gourd of a moon. Did Jonas Renwick know this already, or did he only know sheep and a hate of women? Impatient with herself and her thoughts Maggie switched on the torch and crossed to the old house.

She slept from the moment she climbed into her bed, and she slept all night.

CHAPTER FOUR

MAGGIE awoke to new noises. The soft wash of water had been her good-morning signal for so long that at first she could not sort out the unaccustomed cries that aroused her. She stumbled sleepily to the window and blinked out, at once putting everything into its place. She was west, *very west*, the sounds were the bleats of sheep, and that blurry figure, blurry because she was only half awake, the tender of the sheep. It was Brother Wolf.

She stood staring out at him, and turning unexpectedly, he saw her, and raised an arm. Embarrassed by her sleep-crumpled pyjamas, by her sleep-touselled hair, Maggie edged from the window, grabbed up her housecoat and hurried along to the bathroom. Grandfather called out that a pot of tea waited, so her shower was a quick one.

The old man was clearly pleased to have Maggie around. He put a steaming cup in front of her and began fixing bacon and eggs. No, he said firmly to her objection, if she worked hard at Phineas, and no doubt Jonas would work her very hard, she would need to eat up.

As Maggie did so she heard the whirr of a plane,

by the single sound of the engine the same plane, or similar, to the craft she had watched departing yesterday. Helen's plane.

Grandfather, buttering toast, nodded at her. 'I told you so, didn't I? She comes every day.'

'She may as well work here,' Maggie observed, 'stop here.' She thought a little wistfully that she could do with another woman for company.

'Work isn't what is required,' Grandfather said succinctly, 'but I think stopping is.' He looked meaningly at Maggie, but she pretended not to see. She reminded herself that it was not her concern, that she would not become involved. She kept eating.

Breakfast over, she decided to go across to the store earlier than required so she could look around at what offered, something she had found little opportunity to do last night. She thanked the old man, said it was a fine start to the day, and left the house.

There was a fair variety of goods, she discovered; Jonas Renwick had stocked well. She did not think much of his arrangement, but she supposed he had not found time yet for presentation or display. She set to it herself, so enjoying the task she did not know until Tim Renwick spoke to her that he had come into the shop.

'This is fun!' she told him with enthusiasm after she had returned his greeting.

'But a task I should be sparing you,' Tim said in apology.

'I told you it was fun, Tim,' Maggie said again.

'Then fun I should have shared. I completely forgot the store last night, Maggie. Also I forgot the tour in the afternoon. Now I arrive later than you have. I'm a dead loss—but no doubt Jonas has told you.'

'Not in those words,' Maggie tried to comfort him. 'We all run late some time,' she excused, 'we all forget.' But Tim only sighed.

'It's not such a sin,' Maggie tried again. 'After all, your job is rock, isn't it, not stores, not tours.'

Again Tim did not speak, and, believing he was being humble, she pointed out: 'A rock camp revolves around its geologist.' She felt like adding: 'Not its sheep farmer,' but forbore.

Tim looked at her as though he wanted to tell her something, but when he did speak it was an apology again.

'I forgot,' he said. 'I have ever since——' His voice trailed off.

'The accident?' Maggie asked gently.

'You know about it.'

'Grandfather told me there'd been a tragedy.'

'Yes. Four parents killed—our parents—and Helen's.'

'I've met Helen, Tim,' Maggie told him.

'Well, you had to some time, I suppose,' Tim said a little helplessly. 'She's always here.'

'Why?' Maggie dared ask. 'I mean' ... at Tim's uncertain look ... 'if Helen needs to get out, as she must to come so often, why not some other place? Some place' ... carefully ... 'where she might be more welcome?'

'She's not unwelcome here,' Tim said in-adequately, 'she's just——'

'Just not present,' Maggie suggested.

Tim did not answer that. He kept tidying the piles of paperbacks, and when Maggie went into

the small annexe to get out some more stock, he
left.

It was time to open up, so Maggie did so,
grateful, since Tim did not return to help her, that
the number of customers was moderate, their
requirements simple. She found she could manage
quite well alone. At nine she closed the store again
and reported to the office to ask the boss what to
do next.

Jonas Renwick was sitting at the desk going
through a pile of correspondence, and, after
glancing up, he nodded to a jar of coffee in a
corner, cups, biscuits.

'I take no milk, no sugar,' he directed.

'Yes, sir.' Maggie carried out the order capably;
making the coffee had been one of her old jobs.

When she put the result in front of him he
looked at the singleness, then looked at her.
'Where's yours?' he asked.

'I didn't make any, I didn't know if I was
allowed to indulge with my employer.'

'Indulge?' One eyebrow shot up.

Maggie flushed at her word choice. 'Take a
break,' she substituted.

'You are allowed.' He waited until she came
back with her cup. 'Sleep well?' he asked.

'Yes, thank you.'

'Did you open up the store this morning?'

'On the dot. Business was satisfactory. I would
say. You need more cordial.'

'To take away the taste of the water,' he
grimaced. 'Artesian is not a preferred flavour.' He
looked at her narrowly. 'Did Tim turn up for
duty?'

'Of course.' Maggie hoped she had not said that

too promptly, for his eyes were still narrowed. Yet Tim *had* turned up, she thought.

Jonas must have decided to believe her. 'Good, then,' he accepted. 'If he hadn't turned up this time I would have had his hide.'

'Yes,' Maggie said coolly, 'I expect you would.'

'Yours, too' ... the cobalt eyes still narrowed ... 'if you'd lied for him.'

Praying that a guilty red did not stain her face, Maggie insisted: 'Tim was with me.' She glared back at Brother Wolf.

Jonas took a long gulp of his black brew, then drawled: 'No doubt you enjoyed it.'

'Very much. I like meeting the public.'

'I was speaking of an individual, not the public. I was referring to my brother's company. No doubt you enjoyed it.'

'Very much,' Maggie assured him.

'Even after my warning?' he asked her.

'Warning?' she queried.

'Against getting interested in Tim even though he might appear to be interested in you.'

'Oh, yes, I recall you saying that,' Maggie returned.

'Then act on it,' he said heavily. 'I don't want trouble.'

'Trouble being Tim and me? If I recall rightly yesterday trouble was you and me. It was a Renwick, anyway.' Maggie laughed. Recklessly, she added: 'I must have the de Merril complaint!'

He looked angrily across the desk at her. 'Who mentioned the de Merrils?' he demanded. 'No, don't bother, it was Grandfather. He talks too much, and you listen the same.'

'There's been nothing to listen to,' Maggie

retorted. 'Only innuendoes, half-truths and things partially said.'

'Then leave them at that. You were not signed on to play Miss Marple, Maggie, you are simply at Phineas to look after the guests and serve in the shop. Also' ... glancing around him ... 'you can help me in the office. But your Phineas work goes strictly no further. No espionage. No gossip column.'

'I understand what you require, Mr Renwick,' Maggie said coolly.

'Oh, no, you don't, that is what *Phineas* requires, never me. To my mind there are only two requirements of a woman: the kitchen, the bed.' Before Maggie could expostulate, and she was going to expostulate, he asked: 'What are your other accomplishments? I mean apart from *not* lying on a beach golden and——'

'As well as hostessing I can type, file, calculate,' began Maggie, but he halted her.

'The typing will do at present. I have a few letters drafted out. Tidy up my spelling and make three copies. I have some jobs outside, so I won't be here to see if actually you do type or only hunt around. When you get through you can walk across to the motel, meet the new guests who arrived last night.'

'Did they?' asked Maggie.

'The last of the groups,' he said.

'I had a look at the motel yesterday,' she ventured. 'Helen de Merril was there.'

'Nothing to stop her,' he returned coolly.

'Also nothing to welcome her,' Maggie insinuated.

'Anxious to be Mother Confessor now?' he

pounced. 'Look, Miss Wentworth, it all happened years ago, and when I say "it", don't look confused, because you know all about it, I can tell by your face. Grandfather told you, didn't he?'

'A little.'

'Which stops at a little, as far as I'm concerned. When you've done your chores here, do some hostessing over there.' He strode out.

Maggie typed the letters carefully. She checked, then double-checked them: she wanted them to be perfect. She knew she had no need to 'tidy up' his spelling, but all the same, suspecting a possible trap, she did. As she had thought, he was as meticulous on paper as he had been with his fences for his precious sheep. Jonas, she derided, and his 'babies'.

She put the letters on the desk, then left the office to perform her next chore: the new guests.

She knocked on the door of every unit, and every time a wife answered. The gem-struck husbands were trying their luck already, Maggie gathered, while the women did the settling in.

She chatted amicably with each one. This was work she knew and liked very well. Tourists were easy people to deal with, she had always found. They came to enjoy themselves, and that made her job enjoyable. All the wives assured her that tomorrow they would be out with their picks, too. One optimistically told her she had ordered a huge ruby, another said she would settle for nothing less than the biggest diamond in the world. Maggie, keeping in mind Tim's few instances to date, knew that there would probably be nothing, but it was good fun, and fun, after Brother Wolf, was something she needed.

As the female prospecting was not to start until the next day, Maggie decided to arrange something for the afternoon. She advised them all to take the Phineas Rock Tour as a fitting opener, then, thinking that a little knowledge would do her no harm as well, she resolved to seek out Tim and learn some of the gen.

She located their rock man in the display and sales section that Jonas had had built, yet not so much for the display, Maggie suspected, noting the price tags, as for the sales. There was no doubt that Brother Wolf was after money, she thought. Tim's money. Some of the amounts startled her. How many 'babies' for Jonas would that gem bring?

Tim was examining a stone that he told Maggie was a tourmaline.

'Until now that meant only a Brazilian sapphire,' he said, 'but I've found a couple here at Phineas.'

'What's this, Tim?' Maggie was moving along the counter.

'A topaz. It's a surface gem. The prospectors love those—they're easy digging. Here's an offering of Australian diamonds that Jonas had brought in for display only, as we haven't found any ourselves yet. They're not as large as we would like, Australian diamonds aren't, but the brilliance is unsurpassable. What is your choice of gem, Maggie?'

'I'll tell you after you tell me more about all this,' Maggie urged. 'I've just discovered I'm Project Mother, and such mothers don't always get asked motherly things. I have to be knowledgeable, Tim, so you must tell me the how, when and why. Also the what. What, for instance, is that burner doing?' Maggie had moved to the working end of the bench.

'Its purpose is to test any finds,' said Tim, and he indicated a glass rod, borax and soda. 'You powder a small sample, then sprinkle it on the flame. Reach your conclusions.'

'Are prospectors often disappointed with conclusions?' Maggie enquired. 'I've heard you can be with gold.' She smiled and reminded him: 'Fool's Gold.'

'Yes, they're disappointed quite often, but they still come back again. There's nothing like that sweet, sharp urge nudging at your shoulder when you're on to something.'

'An urge to keep on, Tim?'

'Yes, Maggie. Come and I'll show you.'

About to ask: 'Should we? Mightn't Jonas object to mid-morning excursions?' Maggie went instead. After all, if she was to answer questions, she had to know what to say. She got into step beside Tim.

'Years ago,' Tim told her as they crossed the dry Reptile River, 'all a prospector would have brought along would have been a dish and a dolly pot. He would have swished the water around, looking for tin, wolfram, platinum, and of course——'

'Gold,' finished Maggie.

Tim smiled at her enthusiasm. 'I believe you're feeling that sweet, sharp urge nudging you already.'

'I am.' Maggie half turned to look around her. 'Tell me more about gold,' she begged.

'Well, in spite of your Fool's Gold, Maggie, you

can't really reach a wrong conclusion with gold. Gold looks like gold, feels like gold, is the colour of gold. In fact it is gold.'

'Could there be any here, Tim?' she asked.

'Gold can be anywhere, even in sea-water.' Tim was ahead of Maggie now, and she had to run to catch up. Enthusiastically she suggested to him that he included all this in today's tour.

'Tour—?' At once she could see that Tim had already forgotten. He did not admit it, though.

'Bring in the Brazilian sapphires, the topazes, the sweet, sharp urge,' she persuaded. 'If I've found it enthralling, the tourists will, too.'

'You really think it will go down?'

'Perfectly.'

'Good, then,' he promised. 'Over the hill' . . . he smiled remindingly at her . . . 'are more items. Come and I'll show you.'

'No,' declined Maggie, feeling a pang of conscience, 'I'll take the geologist's word.'

Tim never answered that, and, on some impulse, Maggie turned to look at him. She was struck by the expression on his face. There was a reluctance there. An uncertainty. Uneasy over both, Maggie prompted: 'You *will* turn up this afternoon?'

'Of course,' Tim said.

'Then I'll go back to the office now. I've already been away too long.' Maggie returned.

All the morning, in spite of having heard the Cessna's arrival, Maggie had caught no glimpse of Helen de Merril. Over lunch later with Grandfather she spoke about this.

'It's always like that, Maggie,' Grandfather said. 'The girl could be anywhere—reading under some tree, sitting by the creek, hunched in the cockpit ready to leave again.'

Grandfather was not chattering so much, Maggie observed, so she did not talk, either. After the meal was finished, she did a quick tour of the camping and caravan areas, again urging Tim's tour to anyone there to listen.

After that she went to the office.

Again Jonas was away, but he had provided her with more letter drafts. She worked intently for an hour, then, glancing out of the window, she was perturbed to see a small crowd gathered outside the store, which was almost opposite. The shop was not due to open until the evening, so why were all those women there now? Maggie asked.

At once, sickeningly, she recalled the tour. It should have left by now, but going by the waiting crowd, who could not be waiting for anything else, it had not. Without any doubt Tim had forgotten again.

Maggie got up from the typewriter and hurried by a back way to Tim's work bench in the display and sales room.

'Tim!' she called.

He was not there.

She stood tapping her foot for a moment, wishing he would return from wherever he had taken himself. A glance at her watch told her that already ten minutes had elapsed since she had noticed the crowd outside the store, and only they knew how long they had waited already. From her courier days Maggie knew that guests did not take kindly to being forgotten.

She called louder for Tim, no result, then turned unhappily and went across to the meeting place.

What am I to say? she was asking herself? What can I do?

But for the fact that one of the tourists, seeing her, called: 'At last!' Maggie would not have thought of doing what she then did, and that was conduct the tour herself.

Quite calmly, though she could not have said how when she knew so little, she herded the group together and led them where Tim had led her. That part was easy, leading tourists was her stock-in-trade . . . except that in this instance she was quite ignorant about the stock.

She did her best, though, she repeated everything that Tim had told her, and because the sweet, sharp urge of finding something was affecting them, too, the tour was a success.

But a success with a flaw for Maggie. In her heady satisfaction with herself and her performance, Maggie led the group up the 'hill' she had not yet climbed. Everything would be the same over the other side, she thought, the same as it was this side of the slope, and that was red, sandy, rocky, featureless, and stretching for ever.

It was like that, so how, Maggie asked herself later, did she manage to get lost? Lost in an ochre world of nothing at all except wind indentations and brooding endlessness.

She talked even more brightly when she realised the position, she said everything Tim had said, not for a moment did she falter, let anyone suspect that she had not the least idea where she had led the group, or how in heaven she was to get them back.

The first shadows were creeping in now, and Magie was resigning herself wretchedly to the fact that she must come to terms and confess what she had done. It was then that something did nudge her, nudge very forcibly, and it was no sweet, sharp urge, it was——

'Tim—thank heaven!' Maggie exclaimed in relief.

'Not quite. Look again.' The voice was soft. 'Well, ladies' . . . in a louder voice . . . 'have you had a good tour? Have you enjoyed yourselves? I trust Project Mother hasn't pushed you too much. Are you ready to return?'

Yes, they were ready, they agreed. It had been most interesting.

'I'll take you back a shorter way than you came, so you may still make the hot showers before your menfolk. Follow me, please.'

Maggie, with the others, followed *Jonas* Renwick.

When they reached the project, Jonas dismissed them . . . with the exception of Maggie. 'Before *you* shower,' he said softly and only for her again, 'I want to see you in my office. Good afternoon . . . no, it's good evening, isn't it? Anyway, ladies, now that you know all about it, no doubt you'll be beating your men in the gem game.' He laughed pleasantly at them.

Quite won over, they laughed back, suspecting nothing, promising they would.

'I'll be watching you,' Jonas promised in his turn, using his cobalt charm successfully on them, but at the same time compelling Maggie in the direction he required.

When the two of them reached his office, he opened up, gave Maggie a hard push in, then entered himself.

He slammed the door.

CHAPTER FIVE

'You damn conceited little idiot!' Jonas began violently. 'You fool! What did you plan to do? Ruin everything? Ruin me? Where would Phineas have stood after parting out compensation to twenty-five husbands for the loss of twenty-five wives?'

Maggie included pathetically: 'And me.'

'No loss,' he cancelled.

'I told you,' he continued, 'that I'd have Tim's hide if he didn't take stock of himself, so seeing he hasn't, I will, the moment we meet up.' The cobalt eyes glinted at Maggie. 'But I told you as well, didn't I, and we are meeting now, so by heaven——' He took a step forward and Maggie took a step back.

To gain time she agreed with him. 'Yes, I have been an idiot. But—conceited?'

'You were showing off,' he accused. 'You were out to prove that in one day a new chum—*you*—could know what it takes most men their entire life to learn.'

'The west?' Maggie barely breathed it, but he still heard her and stepped forward again, this time to take her arm with such a hard grasp she could not withdraw.

'Yes, the west, and particularly this part of it. It can still baffle the old hands, yet you, a bikini hostess——'

'At least you're clothing me now!' Maggie broke

54

in furiously. 'Before, it was——' She reddened and grew silent.

'It was golden and naked on a beach,' he finished for her, and he gave a dry laugh.

'My work was not all done on a beach,' Maggie defended.

'Work?' he interrupted, and again he laughed.

'I was expected to be alert, responsible. I remember heading a party one time——'

'In a conga?' he interrupted next.

'In a tour of exploration up the coast.'

'Don't tell me, let me guess,' baited Jonas. 'You got lost. You're trying to tell me that what happened today can happen in other places as well.'

'Yes,' admitted Maggie unwillingly, 'but I'm also trying to tell you that on that occasion I coped.'

He looked incredulously at her. 'How could you not cope,' he pointed out, 'when you had only to climb a cliff or shin up a palm tree to find out where you were? Here, in case you haven't noticed, are none of those aids. Yes, an idiot,' he said again.

Maggie thought bitterly that she was indeed an idiot ever to have abandoned cliffs and palm trees. She wished intensely she was back there again. She supposed Jonas was wishing the same.

He did not say it, though. At the moment he was saying nothing, he was staring broodingly ahead.

'Is it that important?' she dared to break in.

· 'My near ruination? The close loss of everything I've worked for? Of course.'

'Tim worked, too,' she reminded him. 'In fact I

would call Tim the real motive of it all—the heart.'

Jonas was taking out his pipe, that pipe he seemed to finger but not smoke.

'How?' he asked rudely.

'Rock is the sole reason these people have come here,' Maggie challenged.

'Go on,' he nodded.

'Well, money from them is what you were, and are, after. For your sheep.'

'For my improvement of them—I admit it. But who began the guest business in the first place? Who instigated it? Certainly not Tim.'

'Not ostensibly, perhaps, and not in practice. But he is the inspiration—he has to be. Your paying guests only came because of the rock, and Tim is the rock. To my mind such stimulation is far more important than—well, driving in a nail, or stocking up a shop.'

'Lilies before butter, you really mean. Or in this case wouldn't it be silly, useless little stones before——'

'Sheep,' rushed in Maggie angrily. 'It always comes back to sheep!'

'I was going to say life,' he shrugged, 'but seeing everything that breathes is life—*and flesh and blood*' ... his eyes flicked a tacit reminder ... 'sheep will do.'

'The tourists are only here because of what Tim has to offer them,' Maggie said hastily, anxious to avoid that cobalt reminder.

'Then why the hell wasn't Tim offering it this afternoon?' Jonas demanded. 'Yesterday? Any damn time? And why the hell are you defending him?'

'I'm not, I'm only pointing out——'

'Then I'll do some pointing out, too. If it were left to Timothy nothing would ever get done. Oh, I admit it's the rock that's bringing in the shekels at present, but that's my doing, never Tim's.'

Maggie looked at him despairingly. 'You should try to understand your brother, make allowances that he's different stuff from you. That he's a dreamer.'

'Then it's time he woke up from that dream!'

'I still think,' Maggie persisted, 'that without Tim's knowledge——'

'Knowledge!' Jonas looked at Maggie . . . then he looked away.

Maggie waited, puzzled, for a while, then said: ''You don't move with the times, do you? You want this country back to what it was a century ago.'

'That's true,' he nodded. 'Unspoiled by picks and crash hammers.'

'Then why——'

'Why have I begun this gem stunt? One: because I have an aged grandparent to support. Two: because I have a dreamer ditto. *Your* dreamer. Three: because I know all I do won't be wasted.' Unexpectedly Jonas's attitude completely altered. He came closer to Maggie and he confided in a different voice: 'I, too, have a dream, Maggie. The buildings I have had erected here will one day be in *proper* use, the rooms filled with *real* men, country men, not city prospectors playing at get-rich-quick.'

'That is your dream?'

'Yes.'

'Wall-to-wall on the floor for your shearers?'

'Why not?' he came back at her.

There was silence for a few moments. Then:
'Two Renwick dreamers,' Maggie remarked.

When he did not comment, Maggie went back
to her misadventure. Again she said she was
sorry .

'But I do know the rules of survival,' she said
proudly. 'How to trap moisture, the importance of
remaining at a base, the——' her voice trailed
away at his look of contempt.

'So our girl from the beach knows all the
answers!'

'Some of them.'

'Damn few of them. None of us do. Even my
brother, who boasts he can trace back this country
for a million years.'

'Tim doesn't boast, and it's sixty million.'
Maggie added: 'Tim told me that.'

'Words from the expert?' Jonas asked.

Maggie looked levelly at Jonas. It was none
of her business, but she was still going to ask.

'Why,' she said, 'do you hate him so much?'

There was an instant silence, and it was a long
while before Jonas broke it.

'I?' Another silence. 'Hate Tim?'

'I'm sorry,' Maggie said wretchedly. She knew
she should not have trespassed. It seemed it was
not to be her day.

'That's all right,' Jonas accepted. 'I admire
loyalty, even when it's directed against me. But I
would have more admiration if in the future you
would keep your loyalty to yourself, stop in your
own base. Where' . . . he looked at his watch . . .
'you should be right now.'

'What do you mean?' Maggie asked.

He showed her his wrist. 'Eight o'clock, Miss

Wentworth. The store.'

'But it can't be that late,' disbelieved Maggie.

'It will be by the time you open up.'

'I haven't had my evening meal,' Maggie said mutinously.

'A shame,' he agreed.

'It will be a shame for Grandfather, he takes great pains.'

'A pain in vain tonight. I'll call in and tell him so, tell him to keep whatever Cordon Bleu dish he's concocted either hot, or serve it tomorrow night. Will that do?'

'I'll be hungry,' Maggie complained.

'Then don't open any biscuits,' he advised unkindly. 'Out here it's a long way to replenish stores. Also, if you do, I shall know. I count the packets.'

'I'm sure,' said Maggie. She turned to the door. 'Then I'll go.'

'I'm expecting you to,' he replied as she went.

She crossed slowly to the trading post. She still could not credit that it was time for the night opening. She must have been out in the wilderness much longer than she had thought. She gave a little shiver as she recalled how she had felt when she had first realised she was lost . . . and twenty-five souls with her. However, the ladies had seemingly not noticed, and certainly Jonas had saved the situation with his apparent casual acceptance of the episode. Afterwards it had been much less casual. What a hard, bitter man he was!

Yet for a moment, Maggie remembered, those cobalt eyes of his had dreamed instead, and the dreamer had *not* been bitter. What had Jonas said? 'One: I have an aged grandparent to support. Two:

I have a dreamer. Three——'

'Maggie!' greeted Maggie's original dreamer, and Maggie emerged from her own dream to smile at Tim.

Tim did not smile back. Instead he despaired of himself: 'What can I say? What have I done?'

'Say nothing, Tim.' Maggie took pity on him. 'Nothing has been done.'

'No credit to me,' Tim persisted. He looked so thoroughly miserable Maggie crossed to him and gave him an encouraging shove.

'Snap out of it, Tim. I think we're gong to be busy.' She indicated a small crowd.

'I feel so awful, Maggie, so inadequate.'

'Tim—please! The customers are waiting. You take the book section, I'll manage the rest.'

'Afterwards can we talk, Maggie?'

'Yes,' Maggie promised him, and for the next hour she saw Tim only between sales, which Jonas should find very satisfactory. It was a good night.

But at last the final customer left, and Tim shut the door.

At once he crossed appealingly to Maggie. 'Bawl me out,' he begged. 'I'd feel better.'

'I have no doubt your brother will do that,' Maggie assured him.

'I'll deserve it for today and every other occasion I've let him down,' groaned Tim. 'But this time was the worst. Yet I did intend to make a fine tour of it, Maggie, *I did*, after all, it's something I like. But then——'

'But then an absorbing instance of quartzite intervened?' Maggie suggested gently.

There was a pause, then: 'I suppose so,' Tim agreed.

'Suppose——' Maggie looked curiously at him.

'No, of course it did,' he amended at once. 'Anyway, when I did remember, it was too late. You were home again. But, hell, Maggie, what would I have done if anything had happened to you out there?'

'Also to twenty-five others,' Maggie supplied.

'It was you I was thinking of,' Tim murmured as he came closer to her.

At the same moment Maggie leaned forward and switched off their electricity. She knew power from a home plant was a precious commodity and never to be squandered. As her finger pulled down the button Tim reached her side. All at once it was dark, so dark that she could not see him, but she could sense his near-presence, she could hear his uneven breathing. Evidently he was still upset. Poor Tim!

'Maggie,' she heard him saying, 'I've always been a loss.'

'Oh, Tim——' she tried to placate.

'It's true. Ask Jonas. Ask Grandfather. I've never pulled my weight. I've wanted to, but——'

'You're different, Tim,' Maggie endeavoured.

'All the same I'm a failure. it came after the accident, ever since then——'

'Don't think of it, Tim, don't brood over it.'

'I have to. *I have to*, Maggie. It's always there, you see.'

Impulsively she stopped him with the only weapon she could think of: her lips against his. The next moment he had his arms around her. The kiss he gave her was as gentle as hers had been.

Then quietly he left.

Gathering her own things in the darkness,

Maggie followed him. As she shut the door behind her she saw that Tim had already gone.

'Everything locked up?' Jonas Renwick came out of some shadows to test the door.

'Of course,' said Maggie. 'Goodnight.' She started across to the homestead, only to find him barring her path.

'Hungry?' he enquired.

'Well, I did miss my tea.'

'Yet you satisfied your other hunger quite satisfactorily?' he asked next.

'What are you talking about?' Maggie asked.

'Think it over,' he advised.

'No,' snapped Maggie, incensed, '*you* do that.'

'On this side of a glass I don't need to think.' he pulled her masterfully to where she knew now he must have been standing, then directed her glance to the shop she had just left. The moon was up, and it was shining directly into the store. It was shining where she and Tim had stood.

'You were watching us,' Maggie said distastefully.

'Not at all, you imposed yourselves on me,' he returned.

'I don't like being spied on,' Maggie said resentfully.

'But you like, it's apparent, other things,' Jonas suggested.

'You're hateful!' she snapped.

'But correct?' he waited a moment. 'In which case,' coming nearer to her, 'try my variety of kisses, Miss Wentworth.' He had her in his arms on his last word, and from then on Maggie stood locked in those arms, breath-close to him. She remained so close-locked she was sure she would suffocate as his lips found hers, then commanded them, forced and demanded them, to return what he was giving to her. In the end, to make it more bearable for her, she did.

At once Jonas released her, even gave a little laugh as he did.

'See, it wasn't so hard, was it?' he asked. 'Even when it was not your dreamer but Brother Wolf?' He gave a mock bow, and left her standing there.

Unsteadily Maggie walked across to the homestead, stumbling a little on the uneven ground since she had no torch to light her path.

But on the verandah Grandfather held up a guiding lantern, and, controlling herself with difficulty, Maggie called as brightly as she could: 'Ahoy there—I hope you kept me some supper.'

'Piping hot,' he called back, 'so come and eat it while you tell me all about it.' Over his shoulder as he led her down the hall to the kitchen he added: 'Tell me what he's done this time.'

'He?' Maggie was sniffing hungrily.

'My grandson. What is it, Maggie? Tell me the worst.'

CHAPTER SIX

'SOMETHING happened, didn't it?' Grandfather put a steaming plate in front of her. 'Jonas called in to tell me to hold dinner back, so I guessed at once.'

Before Maggie could speak, he continued, 'He's a worry, that fellow, and just now an extra worry because he's worrying you. But don't you let him,

Maggie. It's Renwick trouble, not yours.'

'It has to be mine, too,' Maggie pointed out, 'when I'm so much on the scene.'

'Then don't be,' Grandfather advised.

'When he employs me?'

'Who—Timothy?'

'Oh, Grandfather!' Maggie, in spite of her recent rage, found herself laughing. 'We're talking about different men.'

For the first time since she had come here Grandfather did not join in her mirth. Instead his old face was serious. 'Never Jonas,' he told her firmly.

'Then?'

'The other, of course.'

'Tim.' Abstractedly, for all her appetite, Maggie began toying with her food. Yes, she conceded unwillingly, Tim might pose a few problems. To a strictly practical man like Jonas an instinctively sensitive man like Tim could arouse irritation, and from a biased grandparent, for certainly Grandfather was that, there would be a similar result. But for herself, never. My problem, rankled Maggie, is not a dreamer but a wolf.

'What happened, Maggie?' Grandfather was asking her, and a little wearily Maggie told him, regretting that she had to include poor Tim.

'It's easy to forget,' she concluded.

Grandfather permitted her defence, but he still gave her a warning.

'Never, for anyone's sake, play games with our west,' he cautioned.

'He made such a mountain out of it,' Maggie muttered mutinously under her breath. 'He needn't have bawled me out that much.' She believed she had said it to herself, but soon found she hadn't.

'*Tim* did?' Grandfather asked slyly.

'No, a different man.'

This time they both laughed.

'I'm glad you were bawled out, Maggie,' said Grandfather, 'because you deserved it.'

'Perhaps I did, but did it have to be by *him*?'

'You couldn't have been censored by anyone worthier—Jonas is absolutely reliable, absolutely dependable, absolutely——'

'Absolutely unlikeable.' This time Maggie spoke successfully under her breath. Aloud she asked: 'But Tim isn't reliable?'

'Well, you saw what happened today.'

'Yes, I saw ... but what I didn't see, and know nothing about, is what happened *then*? Years ago?' Maggie had put down her knife and fork to look directly across the table at Grandfather. Though it was not her concern, all at once she knew that if she was to stay here, make her contribution here, she had to understand more than she understood now. She wished she had questioned Kathy more closely, but her transfer from Compass Bay to Phineas had only taken a week, merely time for packing and goodbyes. Also the last thing she had anticipated had been a mystery. Yet here she was confronting one.

'Grandfather,' she prompted as the old man did not respond, 'please tell me.'

For a while she did not think he would, then he sighed and did.

'All I can pass on to you, Maggie,' he prefaced, 'is the little I know myself.'

'Then I would be grateful for that.'

The old man nodded, pushed aside his plate, and began to talk.

'My son and his wife and the boys lived here between living in the city.'

'Yes, you told me they preferred a busier life.'

'I believe William would have abandoned Phineas entirely,' Grandfather continued, 'but the property was too big and too potentially valuable for that, so instead, as heir, he divided up his time between there and here.'

'Bringing his family with him?' Maggie asked.

'Bringing Linda and Timothy. Jonas insisted on staying with me, and as Mary had died I was glad of the company.'

Maggie nodded. She asked next: 'Where did the de Merrils come in?'

'Maxim de Merril had included Australia in a world tour his parents had given him when he reached maturity. But after he got out here he never left again. He'd been reared in a world of ordered, cloistered beauty, and I suppose to a young man like Maxim Australia was a challenge. He stayed on here. He married here, had a child here.'

'Helen?'

'Yes. Then he met William, and they became friends. Tea, Maggie?'

Maggie said yes and waited until Grandfather sat down again.

'Maxim was keen on flying,' Grandfather went on.

'Like his daughter? I mean, his daughter is like him?'

Grandfather said yes again.

'William brought him here one weekend and at

once he took to the place. I think it was the perfect
flying . . . big country, big skies, even weather. He
bought a small property some hundred miles out—
not to run it, you understand, Maggie, but to fly
around it. There was no shortage of money there;
there isn't now. Like William, he had city interests,
and, the same as William, came west every month.
Most times he flew here, but when the accident
happened he wasn't flying. He was in William's
car, and his wife and daughter were, too.'

There was a long silence.

'All I can tell you after that, Maggie, is the ring
of a telephone, then a voice breaking the news to
me that four had been killed, three spared. That's
all.' Grandfather took up his cup.

Maggie leaned over and touched the old hand.
'How long ago?' she asked.

'Seven—eight years. I know the two younger
ones were verging on adolescence. It was a very
wrong time for them.'

Is there a right time? Maggie thought.

Aloud she said: 'So both the boys became your
boys, Grandfather? You've told me that Jonas
always was.'

'Yes, I had two new sons. But at once I had
trouble with Timothy. I suppose Linda had spoiled
him. On the other hand, I might have expected too
much after the other one.'

Maggie did not comment on that.

'Whatever it was I could never understand him.
Sometimes I think I never shall,' he sighed.

'When I picked up the children from the
hospital where they'd been taken for medical
checking the doctor warned me that Timothy was
especially affected, that he seemed to be in some

trauma which only time would take care of. I was advised to keep him at home.'

'You mean no school?'

'Only correspondence, Maggie,' Grandfather replied.

'But he did quite wonderfully,' Maggie reminded him. 'A geologist!'

Grandfather gave a faint smile. 'But Tim is not. Rock is only another of the many things that he's taken up eventually to put down again,—as he will put this fad down again in time. He always does.'

'Did Jonas go to school?' Maggie asked next.

'Oh, yes. Jonas was always a man. A little man before the accident, all man afterwards.'

'He was older,' Maggie said impatiently.

'Yes, Jonas was older,' Grandfather agreed.

There was another silence. Maggie waited a while, then broke it.

'And what about Helen?' she asked.

'After it happened Maxim's parents sold up their estate in the Bavarian Alps—Jonas knows where it was. They came out here for the sole and specific reason that Helen was Maxim's child, and since Maxim had become Australian, Helen must be, too. In every way. That's how they thought about things, the manner they believed they should be done.'

Maggie said: 'It must have been a shock to them after green mountains.'

'I often thought that, but I never knew. No one did. They simply stayed on in their son's place, minding it, you could say, for Helen.'

'Proud people.' Maggie was touched.

Grandfather nodded.

'Was Helen sent to school?' she questioned.

'No, she had lessons by mail, the same as Timothy.'

'Did the children ever have them together?'

Now there was the longest silence of all.

'They never ever came together,' Grandfather said. 'Not any more.'

'Not after that night?'

'No.'

'But you can't be serious!'

'I am.'

'But why—*why*?'

'Maggie girl, I've told you all I know.'

'But Helen flies here now. She lands here.'

'And takes off again, flies home. Phineas is the only place for her to fly to, the rest are too far. So' . . . Grandfather spread his hands . . . 'where else?'

'But doesn't anyone ever go down to the paddock?' Maggie was still incredulous.

'I think Jonas did when she first started to come here, but that was almost a year ago. I know he cleared the ground for safety for her. But no one else . . . if you're meaning Tim, and she never comes in her turn. Not actually to us. That is why I know so little about her, and there are things I would like very much to know. Whether she's still affected, as sometimes I think Timothy is. It could be expected, Maggie. You see' . . . a pause . . . 'the two younger ones were awake.'

'Awake?' she queried.

'The time of the accident. You see, it was in the night.'

'Then that would be worse,' Maggie agreed. She was quiet for a few moments, then she asked: 'Who was driving the car, Grandfather?'

Grandfather said: 'My son.' There was misery in his voice.

'But it wasn't his fault,' Maggie said gently. 'You can't, and you mustn't, think that.'

'No, I don't, and I didn't, and I don't believe they did . . . not then.'

'They?' she queried.

'The de Merrils. But in the years after, these last years——'

'Yes, Grandfather?'

'The de Merrils have changed, Maggie. You see, Helen grew into a woman, and the old people had to face that. Face the fact that their own span was nearly over, and that Helen would eventually be left alone.'

'Many women are left alone,' Maggie pointed out.

'Left alone *unprepared*. All the de Merrils did was protect Helen, never prepare her. I believe they realised that, but too late. I think' . . . Grandfather looked at her with meaning . . . 'they want her settled.'

'You mean married?' Maggie asked directly.

'Yes.'

'To a Renwick?'

'Why not?' said Grandfather painfully. 'A Renwick orphaned her, didn't he?'

'Grandfather, don't talk like that!' she protested.

'You're right—I shouldn't. But thinking with a de Merril mind, apart from a Renwick who else is there here?'

'Many right now, because of the project.'

'But none before, and that was when it all began.'

'No,' agreed Maggie. She asked thoughtfully: 'What about Helen? Would she feel the same?'

'I don't know—I told you that. No one knows about Helen except Helen. Just as no one knows about Tim save Tim. And now, Maggie, finish your dinner, then get to bed.'

'Yes,' said Maggie. She got up and kissed him, then padded down the hall, and was soon pulling up the rugs.

But not to sleep. Instead she lay wide-eyed in the charming old room, glad for Grandfather that his wife had been spared all this. To lose two so tragically would have been hard to bear, but the knowledge that two more had gone with them would have been worse.

She thought of the three survivors, but mainly of two of them—Timothy and Helen. They had both been awake, Grandfather had said, on that terrible night. But Jonas, Maggie had gathered, had slept.

She thought of William Renwick, who had driven the car, and the delayed de Merril feeling against him that Grandfather was suggesting. The debt they wanted paid. It was all beyond belief . . . yet believable. Why else did a girl fly here every day?

It was all so bewildering that sleep eluded Maggie, and she knew when she crossed to the office in the morning that her weariness showed. She hoped that Jonas was out, he had been yesterday, but no, he was there, she found.

'You're late,' he greeted.

'Not very—barely five minutes. I was a bit late getting up.'

'Then you should be refreshed, but you look the

opposite. Did you lie awake thinking over your sins?'

Maggie was still caught up in last night's revelations, and, recalling that two children had been awake one terrible night but one had slept, she insinuated: 'Sleep can be handy.' At once she could have bitten out her tongue. Now he would know what she and Grandfather had been discussing.

He did.

He glared across his desk at her, cobalt eyes slitted, mouth pulled thin. He did not speak. The silence became unbearable, and Maggie found she had to break it.

'What do you want me to do this morning?' she asked.

He answered her at once.

He said: 'I want you to clear out. I want you back on your beach again. I want you anywhere else but here. You've been gossiping, haven't you—you're always gossiping, trying to find out the where, why, how.'

'I haven't,' defended Maggie hotly, 'but I would prefer my beach, too. When can I go?'

'When there's a charter available, and heaven knows when that will be, not with the rush that's on now. No, you're stuck. And so, by heaven, am I—with you!' Jonas got up from his desk so violently he upturned a chair. Although he must have heard its impact he did not right the chair.

'Do any damn thing you want to do!' he flung at her as he left the room.

Maggie went to the window and watched him stride across the square, then disappear into the alfresco sections. Woe betide any camper or caravaner who had not obeyed the project rules, she thought. She decided to tidy her desk drawer, but soon realised she was making a haphazard job of it. Instead she began some filing.

Then, all at once needing urgently to get away from it all, she shut the filing cabinet and soon after shut the door as she crossed over to the motel. She would see if any of the wives who had not accompanied their husbands needed occupation. She tapped on each door, but found all the guests away. Gem fever, she shrugged.

At that moment she heard the now-familiar throb of Helen's small aircraft. She stood irresolute for a moment, then, suddenly very resolute, she decided that this was an opportunity she could not miss.

Whether Helen wanted to talk to her or not, Maggie was determined to find Helen, and talk herself. Ask.

The Cessna sat on the end of a runway not even marked by the white upturned buckets often used in the west. It was only a small craft, but it still made the girl half hidden in the cockpit look almost miniature. Certainly not old enough, not strong enough, to handle the machine, Maggie thought, and, perceiving she was as yet unnoticed, she stood a moment studying Helen.

She was very pretty, she decided, but she also lacked any animation. She could have been a china doll sitting there, lovely to look at, but china.

Her scrutiny finished, Maggie gave a little cough, and at once the china doll turned and saw her. Before she could say anything Maggie burst in eagerly:

'I'm so glad you're here, Helen, I just couldn't

stand it any longer—I've been used to people around me, and I've yearned to talk. And talk. Oh, yes' . . . again before Helen could break in . . . 'Grandfather talks, the Renwicks, but I need woman talk, I've really missed that. Most of our tourists were women, and though at times I believe I got too much chatter, these last few days I've felt a void.' Maggie kept her mouth open to continue the outburst before Helen could disappear before her eyes, but this time Helen did manage to insert some words.

'There's a number of women here,' she said expressionlessly. 'I've seen them.'

'Then you wouldn't see them now, or probably tomorrow, the day after. They're by their husbands' sides, prospecting. Anyway, they're married women, so not in my category.' A pause, but not long enough to permit Helen to come in. '*You* are, though.'

'Yes, I'm unmarried.' Helen made the statement in a rather odd voice. It sounded almost as though she wanted to follow up her words, but when Maggie looked at her, the pretty face was blank.

'Then can we talk?' Maggie wasted no time. 'Can I climb up beside you?'

'It would be too hot. I was about to climb out myself.'

'Then do climb out and we'll go somewhere. The homestead verandah? The office?'

'Shouldn't you be working?' Helen asked.

'Not at the moment. Mr Renwick went out unexpectedly' . . . very unexpectedly was the right description . . . 'and he looked as though he wouldn't be back. I did a duty call on the units to see if anyone needed entertainment, but they were all entertaining themselves digging up jewels, or doubtless they hoped. No, Helen' . . . again before Helen could object . . . 'I can legitimately be with you if only you'll be with me.' Maggie put pleading into her voice. 'I'm feeling lonely today,' she sighed.

It was a try that came off. Helen opened the door of her craft and slid down.

'I know loneliness,' she said, but she left it at that.

'Up to the homestead?' Maggie asked.

Helen glanced to a huddle of eucalypts spilling a thin but pleasant shade by the dry creek. 'That will do,' she said tonelessly. 'I'm not stopping long. I just needed to get away for a while. They never mind.' She began walking to the lace of shadows, and Maggie followed her.

They sat down when they reached there, but neither spoke for several minutes. Maggie was about to break the quiet when Helen began again.

'You won't find me any company,' she warned.

'I do, though,' Maggie assured her. 'Thank you.' At once she continued before the small interchange could dry up. 'I told you before, Helen, but I must say it again now: I admire you tremendously. To be able to fly! To climb into clouds and to look down, not up!'

A brief smile lit Helen's face; it was the first time Maggie had seen her smile.

'It is good,' she agreed, 'and I love it. Sometimes I think it's the only thing I have. I know I couldn't bear it without it.'

Resisting a temptation to question 'It?' Maggie asked instead: 'Your family don't mind?'

'No—I just told you. I had to have something,

and they could see I could manage. Even as a child I was mechanically-minded. I should have been a boy. That would have been better for everyone.'

'But not for you, Helen. You must know you're extremely pretty. Women do.'

'I only know what a woman must achieve,' Helen said dully.

'Marriage?' dared Maggie. 'But I think you know that only from your grandparents, don't you? I think achievement would never come into it, not with you, only love.'

Helen turned large startled eyes on Maggie. 'You know nothing about me,' she said.

'No, I don't,' Maggie nodded, annoyed that she might have stopped something before it even started. 'Please, Helen, I just want to talk. Can't we talk?'

Helen paused a moment, then said yes.

'You know out here.' Maggie looked around her.

'I should do. I've been around this part of the west a long time of my life.'

'I know that. You've been here ever since——'

'Since the accident, yes. No doubt you heard about it.'

'It was terrible, and I'm sorry.'

Helen said almost without expression: 'It was a long time ago.'

'Since when,' Maggie inserted, 'you've remained here. You never even went to a school.'

'If you know all about it why are you asking?'

Again Maggie said she was sorry. 'I was only hoping to find out how you felt.'

'How do I feel? How should I feel? I've been indulged in everything a girl can be indulged in all my life. My grandparents are rich.'

'Also rich in the freedom they give you. You come here every day.'

'It would have to be here—where else?' Helen said sharply.

'Some paddock somewhere the same distance?' Maggie returned.

'No, it had to be here,' Helen repeated. 'My grandparents wanted that. Now you can stop asking questions.'

'Only one more,' Maggie begged.

'Well?' Helen invited.

'It's this: Why do you let them do this to you? Why, Helen?'

Now came the longest silence of all, indeed, Maggie believed the girl would never reply.

But she did. She looked at Maggie, moistened her trembling mouth, then said simply: 'They're old. They came across the world to me, and I love them. I love them very much.'

CHAPTER SEVEN

At least they had talked, Maggie thought as she hurried back to the office in case Jonas had returned. The interchange had been brief and only flimsy conversation, but ice had been broken, and Maggie felt pleased with herself. Especially had she been triumphant over Helen's parting words.

'I must go now—thank you. I feel I've blown away a few cobwebs. One day I'll fly you across to meet my people, then fly you back . . . if you'll care to come.'

'I'll come,' Maggie had replied.

They had nodded to each other and left.

As Maggie entered the office now she heard the plane's throb, and knew that Helen was in flight. It had all been most satisfactory. Something, if only a little, had been achieved. Maggie smiled . . . then switched the smile off.

The wolf was back.

Jonas frowned at her as she entered. Well, what had she expected? A welcoming song?

She spoke before he could.

'I've tidied some drawers, done some filing, visited the motel units to see if any of the guests needed my attention.'

'But fortunately for them you found those guests away,' he nodded.

She elected to misunderstand him and said innocently: 'I hope they're fortunate if they've gone prospecting.'

'They have, but their real fortune is not having a certain guide to guide them.'

Maggie heaved an audible sigh.

'Have you always been like this?' she asked. 'Carrying on a grudge for ever?'

'Have you always been a liar?' he retaliated. 'You were not knocking on unit doors, you went down to the landing paddock.'

'I did both,' Maggie informed him.

'For what reason?' Jonas had risen from his desk and now he crossed the room to stand so near to her she could even feel the warmth of his body. He wore his customary gear of checked shirt and rough cords, but the heat outside must have prompted him to unbutton the shirt, for his firm brown skin was exposed from throat to midriff, and that hard middle showed not even a whisper of flesh under the solid silver buckle of a tightly anchoring belt.

Aware of his eyes on the direction of her eyes, Maggie said quickly: 'Genuine?' To her horror, before she realised it she had put out her hand and actually touched the belt. At once on impact of flesh she withdrew her hand, angry with herself.

'Is the feel that loathsome?' he asked carelessly. 'Yes, of course it's genuine. Everything I have is genuine. I only go in for a genuine article. You could keep that in mind.'

'It seems good silver,' Maggie said breathlessly. The nearness of that hard body beneath the large buckle was doing odd things to her. She could feel a river of sweat beginning to trickle down her spine.

'It's mined around these parts,' he answered inattentively. His eyes were watching her. She could tell he read her acute awareness of him and wished she could control her maddening discomposure.

'So there is a potential after all.' She decided to try patronage on him, but she knew her voice sounded uncertain.

'One silver buckle does not assure potentiality,' he smiled thinly. 'One diamond-ruby-whatever does not portend more crown jewels.' He slipped his thumbs under the silver buckle, indirectly directing her gaze again to it. And to him. Maggie knew he was watching her once more, gauging her reaction. But there was not going to be any.

'You're really resolved that, apart from the tourists, nothing is going to happen here at

Phineas, aren't you?' she demanded.

'No, I'm not, nature is. Nature intended breathing, living things here, not inert. You should follow that, Maggie Wentworth, because you are *very* breathing, *very* living.' His eyes raked her. 'I am myself.' The movement of his thumbs still under the silver buckle fascinated Maggie, and again she felt the river of sweat down her spine. She wished he would step back, the heat of his nearness now was disturbing her. If he didn't step back, she would, and of course he would make some issue of that.

To her relief he changed the subject—and took away the thumbs from the belt.

'How did you find Helen this time?' he asked.

'How do you know I saw her?' Maggie returned.

'I know because I saw you both.'

Yes, you would, Maggie thought. Aloud she said: 'We got on better.'

'I thought so,' he nodded. 'It looked like a happy tea party.'

'There was no tea.'

'But happiness?' he baited. 'But I already know you would be happy, you're always happy delving. What were you after today, Miss Marple? A dead body?'

'If it were yours I would be most happy,' said Maggie with heat, and she stepped back from him. It did not help her, for Jonas advanced a step.

'What's wrong with my body?' he taunted. 'You certainly gave it a long look just now.'

'Of dislike,' Maggie supplied.

Jonas considered that a moment, then he laughed. It was a lazy laugh. 'You know,' he drawled, 'I don't believe you. I believe you were, if briefly, as conscious of my body as I was conscious of yours.'

'Do I hear that from a misogynist?' Maggie asked.

'A woman-hater need not be a life-hater,' he drawled. 'I'm not. I like life, and I like the way nature has arranged for life's continuance. If I dislike the other component to the continuance, it doesn't mean I buck the system. Also' ... stepping back now and taking out his fingering pipe ... 'keep in mind those winds of change. Though you didn't appeal to me at first, things can still happen.'

'Not to me,' Maggie flashed.

'Don't be too sure.' He put out a hand and stopped her as she turned angrily to the door. 'Where are you going?'

'Away. I don't like this brand of talk.'

'But you're not in the position to like or dislike it, are you? You're the employee, I'm the boss.'

'Mr Renwick, I don't want to be employed by you. Not any more.'

'Because I just admired you?'

'If that was admiration——'

'It was not, it was——' He came close to her once more.

'I don't want to hear!' Maggie said a little shrilly, and backed away from him.

'That suits me,' he agreed idly. 'I have something much more pertinent to say to you.' He waited, then: 'Why are you so interested in all of us?'

'I'm not,' denied Maggie.

'After seeking out Helen to probe her?'

'I didn't seek her out for that, I was sorry for the girl.'

'So am I, we all are, but there's no reason for you to be. You're an outsider.'

'Yes,' said Maggie with feeling, 'thank goodness, I'm an outsider.'

A moment went past. It was a long moment. 'You should be thankful,' said Jonas in an unexpected quiet, 'because it was not a happy time, not at all. But also' . . . in a louder, brisker voice . . . 'it won't make it any happier now having you interfere. The thing happened, and four people were killed. Two old folk now believe their granddaughter must be avenged.'

'Avenged?' she echoed.

'Or would you say revenged?' he asked.

'Only if the revenge dealt with you,' Maggie returned. She went to her desk, and, seeing he had given her no task, she resumed the filing she previously had begun.

He watched her narrowly, and she braced herself for another attack.

'It's a different variety of filing you performed on your glamour island, isn't it?' he suggested too-pleasantly. 'It's not quite lying on a beach and attending to red nails.'

'You really are obsessed with that beach.' Maggie smiled too-pleasantly back.

'Would it surprise you if I answered no, only what lies on the beach?'

'Sand,' Maggie informed him impertinently, and, feeling the winner, she watched him stride out of the office a second time.

She worked steadily on the files, not permitting herself even one moment of resentment. If she had let her tight composure falter she knew she would have downed tools at once, walked out. But walk where? As far as she could see stretched endless nothingness, the nearest place was Helen's, a hundred miles away, and as isolated as Phineas. No, she was stuck here until such time as an empty charter plane flew in and she could fly out.

Which she would. Maggie gritted her teeth. Jonas had gone too far this time. Once she found an exit he would never see, or bait, her again.

In spite of double-checking each item so there could be no complaint the filing soon was finished. Maggie supposed she had better visit the guests again.

She found the units still vacant, and, seeking out the cook, learned that an all-day expedition was taking place, that hampers had been provided.

'Sapphires and sausage rolls,' smiled Maggie.

'I think the order was diamonds,' he grinned back.

It was still too early to cross to the homestead for lunch. How would she fill in an hour? She looked around her.

Then, as if by a magnet, she found her gaze compelled beyond the dry creek bed across to the old disused mine. In some way she could not have explained it beckoned her, drew her, and at once she knew that this would be the perfect moment to go and explore it. There was no one around to see her. The expedition,—Tim, she hoped, at its head—would be away for the day. Cook was in his kitchen, Grandfather in his. Jonas—Jonas was anywhere it pleased him, and the farther the better.

Maggie gave a hard look in all directions, then began a devious track to her goal, sometimes hiding behind trees, sometimes crouching under bushes, trying her best not to seem there at all.

She reached the dried-up river. How long, she wondered, had the Reptile been like this? The bed was so seared and cracked she decided that many years had gone by without any stream passing its way. Its surroundings were dry, too, but once, surprisingly, she heard her feet squelch, and, looking down, saw that she had trodden into a moist section. How did moisture occur in such an arid area?

The walk was not an attractive one, indeed it was a little eerie, the stick-dry bushes, the meagre trees, and the sand and gibber depressing. For a moment she even hesitated and looked back at the project. How civilised and welcoming it appeared from here!

Nonetheless she found she wanted to go on. She even knew that if Jonas Renwick had sent scouts out for her she would not have returned. The mine lured her. She had no intention of doing anything foolish, she just wanted to go nearer to it, see for herself. She gave a small smile at that. See what?

She ran the last few yards to the old ghostly rigging, but paused instinctively at the final step. Who had erected this place? she questioned. All she knew was what Tim had said: 'Evidently I wasn't the first rock Renwick, one of my ancestors must have tinkered around, too.'

She looked a long time at the leaning wreck, aware as the minutes passed of a liking for it, not a fear as she might have thought. Friend, she decided, not foe.

But for that friendly feeling she would not have ventured farther, and that was right up to the sagging door to push it. Not for a moment did she expect any response to her push, and she was surprised when the door sighed, then scraped and shoved back.

Maggie stepped eagerly forward, for there was more light inside than she had expected, evidently a part of the roof had collapsed, and now the sun shone in.

But she had no time to spectulate on this. As she stepped, she fell—fell into a hole just beyond the door.

She was not hurt, she felt sure of that, but what instantly alarmed her was the disturbed sandy earth sliding down on her. It was not falling quickly or violently but insidiously and unceasingly. Almost like a thin stream of domestic salt, she thought, or an egg-timer. She was still wondering stupidly about it when she felt sand trapping her ankles, then her knees, then her thighs.

She had not uttered a word since she had fallen in, but now she called out. There was no one to call to, but she knew she had better call while she still could.

The sand had reached her waist now, it was creeping up to her chest, her armpits, but she dared not struggle in case she dislodged more sand and was buried earlier than she otherwise would.

Now the wretched stuff was touching her neck.

Instinctively, as it got to her chin . . . and then her mouth . . . Maggie thrust up an arm. With luck it would protrude if anyone happened along, though who would?

She still kept the arm upright, though, feeling, her face completely in sand now, the beastly grains starting to smother her nostrils and her mouth. Only her fingers remained free, and she fluttered them wildly.

She did not know how long it was before fingers took her fingers, slid them around the curve of a hose, shouted words she could not understand.

There was a long period of pushing and forcing for Maggie, and then miraculously the hose was within reach of her lips. Through its aperture came a harsh voice. 'If you're still alive for God's sake put this in your mouth!'

The voice said it three times before she found she could. At once, blinded with sand, she breathed air again.

But it was a long time later, digging alone and with his bare hands, that Jonas Renwick released her.

CHAPTER EIGHT

MAGGIE opened her eyes to find herself lying on bare earth under a tattered river gum. At no time had she lost consciousness, but her memory of being carried from the old mine to the meagre shade was both vague and sketchy. She could clearly recall arms forcing her upwards from sand that fought to retain her, but after that it was as though she was standing away and watching it all. A dream sequence.

Jonas ... for all her unreality she knew it was Jonas ... must have thought she was dreaming, too.

'Wake up, Maggie!' he directed.

She tried to speak, but it was too awful, her mouth was full of grit. At once he stopped her by stifling her lips with a large brown hand. As he held the hand there he shook his head at her, indicating quiet. When he was satisfied she understood, he began a careful cleaning up.

'There's no water,' he told her, not imposing silence on himself, 'so I'll do what I can until you can get back to a hot bath.' He began on her mouth, using his large handkerchief. 'Not guaranteed sterile,' he regretted, 'but it will make you feel more comfortable, and it shouldn't be too long before you can wash away any germs I've missed.' He wiped each lip gently but firmly; when some sand still adhered he went through the motions again.

Maggie lay docilely enough under his ministrations, but when he parted her lips and began cleaning out her mouth she grunted an objection. He took absolutely no notice of it, he swabbed around inside of her mouth, her teeth, even her tongue. To say the least she found it very demeaning, but that thought was brushed aside in her wonder of what he would do next.

He did her feet, freeing the sand between each toe, tut-tutting as he did. 'Your soles are damp,' he grumbled, 'so mud has formed. You're a dirty little tramp.'

Maggie, recalling the moisture she had encountered on her way to the mine, said: 'I want to tell you something. Can I talk now?'

'You're going to do a whole lot of talking very soon,' he returned, 'but for the moment, shut up!'

Maggie closed her lips. If he did not want to know then she would not tell him. She lay sulkily resigned until she felt him unbuttoning her shirt, then she sat up.

'Don't be a flaming fool!' Jonas pushed her back. 'You're a regular sandbag. I could barely carry you across to this tree, so I certainly don't intend carrying you back to the homestead with a load like that.' He had taken the shirt off by now and was shaking it free, and there *was* a lot of sand.

'Bra now,' he ordered.

'No.'

He did not argue with her, he simply unclasped, removed and shook the article.

He handed it back to her, and she tried to put the thing on again, but it was impossible in her reclining position.

'Allow me,' Jonas said politely, and pulled her upward a few inches and edged the garment over each shoulder in turn. Then, to her fury, he filled each of the cups, even adjusting them. 'Comfortable?' he asked, ignoring her outrage.

What else could he do? Maggie seethed. Well, there *was* more, she knew, but she was not going to permit *that*. She sat right up, her hands going defensively to the zip of her jeans.

'It's all right,' he said in a dry voice, 'I'm not even looking at you. Get up, if you're able, then strip and shake yourself.'

'I'll be all right,' she insisted, 'I'll be able to get back on my own steam.'

'You'll be bogged down. Look, Miss Prim, I'll walk round the mine. By the time I return I'll expect you thoroughly shaken, dressed again, ready for a few pertinent words.' Not waiting for a reply, he left her.

Maggie waited for a few moments to make sure he had gone, then she got up, slid out of her jeans, removed as much anchoring sand as she could, then pulled the jeans on again and zipped them.

She was waiting for him when he turned the last corner of the mine and crossed over.

'You're either prompt or you didn't do a thorough job,' he drawled. 'Did you shake out your knickers as well?'

Maggie did not answer that . . . she could not, and he shrugged and sat down, indicating for her to do the same. When she had done so he began his few pertinent words.

'That was a damn fool thing you did,' he told her. 'You never . . . never, do you hear me? . . . go into any old building, not alone, not without permission. Most of all you never go into a mine. Why did you do it, you crazy girl?'

'I've never been in a mine,' she explained.

'I've never been on a planet!' he snapped.

'I felt attracted by it.'

'Attracted——' Jonas stared at her. 'In all creation, how?' he asked.

'I don't know. I only knew I wanted to go.'

'And what you want you must have, mustn't you? Oh, yes, I've known women like you before.' The bitterness in his voice sent her eyes flashing up to him, but she learned nothing from the cobalt slits, so looked down again.

He did not pursue that line, he asked, still curious: 'What in heaven could a girl like you find interesting in an old mine?'

'I never said interesting, I said——'

'That it attracted you.'

'Yes, but I didn't mean I found it attractive, I meant that it——' Maggie hesitated. She could not say it had lured her, he would only heap more scorn on her, and yet that was what the mine had done. It had compelled her to answer his question, but she gave him no response. After a while he shrugged.

'It doesn't matter,' he said impatiently, 'it's not important, save in the possibility of your having lost your life, which you very nearly did.'

'You care!' she said flippantly, a flippancy that was killed at once with his sour reply.

'Only in the way that such a happening would have caused much inconvenience. I would have had to call in the police to investigate, write endless reports.'

'Poor you,' she proffered falsely, but again was defeated.

'Well, certainly not poor you,' he reminded her, 'seeing you deserved to expire—indeed, you asked for it.'

'But never got it, thanks, sir, to you.' Maggie bowed her head.

'So we're coming round to that, are we?' he said drily. 'To thanks at last.'

Maggie found the grace to say: 'Thank you for saving my life.' She waited a moment. 'But how' ... innocently ... 'did you come to be on the spot to save it?' As though she did not know, she thought, he had found some fault in her filing, and knowing where to find her, as somehow he always knew, he had appeared just in time.

But Jonas's reply surprised her.

'I was at the mine, too. After all, it is Renwick property.'

She started to say: 'So it lures you, too,' but refrained.

'I happened to be there,' he continued, 'and I happened, by sheer luck, to find an odd length of antiquated hose doubtless left there by the last miners. It was mostly perished, but there was still sufficient to shove into some twitching fingers that mercifully I'd seen. My God, Maggie, when I think how near you came to a sandy end . . .' He hit the palm of one of his hands with the fist of the other. 'Your curiosity nearly killed you,' he said, 'so kindly restrict it from now on. Also, now you've experienced what snooping can do physically, it would be well to consider what snooping might do mentally, and I'm not thinking now of you, but others—us, the Renwicks, then Helen. Certainly Helen's grandparents, who could do better, thank you, without your help.'

'How would you know that?' Maggie asked of the last.

'Have they ever invited you to Baden Wald?' he sneered.

'Is that its name?'

'Yes. Have they?'

'Have they ever invited *you*?'

His reply surprised her. 'Naturally,' he said. He waited a moment, then persisted: 'And you?'

Maggie said triumphantly: 'No. But their granddaughter has.'

'What?' Jonas looked at her incredulously.

'Helen has asked me to go over and meet her people, and I intend to.' Before he could break in, Maggie said icily: 'Also regarding my "snooping", as you put it, that word to me conjures up visions of being where I should not be.' She looked challengingly at Jonas.

'Well?' he demanded.

'Well, it was you who recruited me to Phineas,' she reminded him. 'I didn't just arrive here. You asked me to come. You needed me.'

'Perish that thought,' he came in smartly. 'Only the business had a need. Not me. Not for you. And if I'd known then what I know now I would never have opened my mouth. But there's no time for regrets, instead what is all this rot about going across to the de Merrils?'

'I've been asked, and I've accepted,' she shrugged. 'You may be my boss, but you can't order me around on my time off, and it will be during my time off that I snall avail myself of the offer.'

'You will not. Anyway, why do you want to go?'

'To see for myself.' At a dangerous look in his face Maggie amended: 'To relax away from my place of employment for a while. Surely I'm permitted that?'

'You're bored here already?' he asked.

'Would Yes make any difference?' she asked slyly.

'To what?' he asked back.

'My leaving Phineas.'

'None in the world,' he returned. 'You're staying here until I can get you out again.'

'You mean until a charter can take me.—But what if Helen will take me?' That idea had just occurred to her.

'Helen's Cessna has insufficient range,' Jonas told her.

'But Grandfather said that Maxim used to fly from the city.'

'Uncle Maxim was a far more accomplished flier, and he had refuelling tricks that Helen would never know. No, Maggie, don't look to Helen. Anyway' ... a shrug ... 'she wouldn't go.'

Maggie said mutinously: 'We'll see,' and at once received his wrath.

'*We* nothing!' he all but shouted. 'Speak only for yourself because I tell you that girl would not go. Why are you being so damned unreasonable today? First cornering Helen like you did, second coming out here and nearly killing yourself. Now you're saying rash things, idiot things, for you must know you can't leave here without my authority. There's no hope of a charter coming unless I arrange for it, and as for Helen getting you out, forget it. Oh, I know what your poor little brain is thinking, it's that you'll get across to Baden Wald and abandon ship from there. Snare a charter from there. But' ... a mean smile ... 'the Renwicks happen to *own* all these western charters.'

'I should have guessed that,' Maggie sighed. 'Well, I'll walk.'

'And last only hours. That's true. We've actually known it happen since the rain forgot us out here.'

'One thing, I wouldn't be mourned,' Maggie inserted.

'Tim would sigh,' Jonas shrugged, 'he has an eye for what he judged attractive. Grandfather would be sad, he loves you already.'

'But you wouldn't even notice.'

A silence came between them. Then:

'Oh, yes, I would notice, Maggie,' Jonas Renwick said, and he leaned across to her. He waited a moment, then, without any prelude, he took her in his arms and simply held her in them for several minutes—no closer, no farther away. Just held her.

'Relax,' he ordered in a low voice.

'Relax?' Maggie knew she was tense, but despised *him* for knowing it.

'Relax,' he said again, 'because I'm going to kiss you. Ever since I tried it the last time I've been considering doing it again. I wanted to recall the particular taste of you.' Before she could withdraw from him, he was doing what he said. 'My God,' he complained at once, 'you taste of sand, and I thought I'd got all the damn stuff away!' He took out the handkerchief again and passed it over her lips. 'Now,' he said, 'we'll start a second time.'

'No!' Maggie protested furiously, but he paid no heed.

His lips came down on hers, forcing hers to open, exploring her mouth, probing it, running the length of her lips with his own until Maggie felt she must break away or—or——

'Better than the hankie?' Jonas asked in an amused voice.

'You're abominable!'

'Actually,' he corrected, 'I'm very easy-going, I could have cleaned you up *thoroughly* today, not left you to do it yourself. Now' ... his lips beginning to come down again ... 'we'll do it properly, not outrage the tender flower.' He kissed her quietly, but for all the quietness Maggie knew she had never felt so aroused ... or so kissed ... in all her life.

'You are a beast!' she muttered, getting free of him.

'Beasts don't go in for this sort of thing, they start it at once,' he replied.

'Start what?' she asked.

'Don't give me that,' he refused. 'You know what I mean. Don't tell me an island hostess doesn't—couldn't know.'

'Oh, yes, I know, but as it happens I never—I mean——' Maggie stopped, embarrassed.

'Practised it? Good lord, you're all red! Don't tell me it's sunburn. I thought . . . among other things . . . an island hostess would be used to the sun's rays.'

'What we were not used to were brutes!' Maggie stuttered in her anger.

'Brute? Me? Don't suggest that that little play just now was your idea of being brutal. If so, my dear, you've a long, long way to go.'

'But not with you.' In spite of her unsteadiness, for she was still not recovered from her experience, Maggie escaped from him, and began running over the uneven ground in the direction of the homestead.

She did not get far. Fleet as a native runner he came from behind her, and in moments she was on the ground, Jonas, his head supported by his elbows, poised over her, and looking at her quizzically.

'How do you like your eggs cooked now?' he taunted. 'We used to play that at school.'

'This isn't school!'

'No, my God, it isn't.' For the third time he kissed her, but now there was no banter, there was no tender flower treatment either, his hands stopped supporting his head and instead cupped her breasts.

Maggie started to cry, and at once he kissed the
tears. 'Little idiot,' he told her, 'mad, mad girl.'

'But——' she began.

'I was temporarily caught up in the winds of
change,' he reminded her. 'For a few moments I
felt them blowing. They've ceased now, so you can
feel safe, you can get up. But' ... he was on his
feet yet making no attempt to help her to hers ...
'don't ever do what you did today again, or I'll not
only feel those winds, I'll let them direct me.
Strictly from a sensual motive, you must understand, no strings attached, no fine feelings.' He
grinned. 'Consider that a threat, because I know
our Miss Wentworth would never accept it as a
promise.'

'Never,' said Maggie. She had got to her feet
too, and at once she swayed.

Jonas instantly caught her up in his arms, and
began walking. When she protested he said: 'Shut
up, I'm carrying you back. You can run a hot bath
there, but I'm sorry I won't be there to tend to
your bruises, but I've already wasted too much
time on you. After the bath, bed. I'm sorry, too, I
can't help you there, but, being shorthanded now,
I'll have to tend the store tonight myself.'

'Couldn't Tim?' Maggie suggested.

'Leaving me free, you mean?' he misunderstood.
'You tempt me? But aren't you forgetting I'm a
woman-hater?'

'But one,' Maggie flashed, 'with an ear for wind
changes.'

'You would like that tonight?' Jonas looked at
her.

'Certainly not!'

'Then stop talking for the sake of making a

noise,' he said. 'Replying to you doesn't help me at all. You're not a heavy weight, but you're still nicely stacked, and even this short a distance is more than enough.'

'I can walk,' she said.

'And promptly fall over. What would the guests think of me?'

'What will they think of my coming back like this?'

'In my arms, you mean? Presumably that we've been married and I'm carrying you over the threshhold. Now stop wriggling, or, by heaven, you'll have something to wriggle about!'

He strode on, holding Maggie in such a position that she could not prise loose, could not even call out.

Some yards away from the homestead he shouted out to Grandfather who was standing on the verandah.

'Run the bath and make a big pot of tea. There's been a slight mishap—nothing to worry about.'

He carried Maggie up the shallow stairs, then down the hall to the bathroom, where already the bath was beginning to fill.

'A proper clean-up,' he instructed, 'do you hear me? The earth here is considered absolutely pure, even, some say, healing, but grit can be damned irritating if it's not got out.'

'Will you get out?' Maggie shouted at him.

He was looking at her quizzically again, taking in, she thought furiously, every inch of her. 'Do you know what,' he said, 'I want to say back to you, "Gladly I'll get out," but somehow the words just won't come. Why, would you say?' Again he estimated her. 'Those winds of change back?'

Maggie answered thickly: 'Go. Just go!'

Slowly, maddeningly slowly, he went.

CHAPTER NINE

MAGGIE scrubbed the dirt away and with it managed to scrub away some of her anger. By the time she had run a second bath, then soaked in it, she found she could think of other things as well as the embarrassment and indignity Jonas had caused her.

The mine, she began recalling, and she shuddered. It had been very frightening being slowly swallowed up by choking earth, and if Jonas had not come along when he did she would have smothered. She shut her eyes and tried to think of something else.

Of all things damp toes came back to her! Jonas had complained that hers were muddy, but he had not asked her how. She had been going to tell him about stepping into squelchy moisture on her way to the mine, but he had quietened her ... that is if a terse, Shut up! comprised quietening. Maggie grimaced. She decided to dismiss damp toes as unimportant, but she still felt curious about that wet patch. In the middle of this aridity how did moisture occur?

A gentle tap on the bathroom door jerked her out of her introspection. It was Grandfather, anxiously needing assurance that she was all right.

'I'm not drowned, if that's what you mean,'

Maggie laughed back. 'I'm getting out now, and dressing. It must be time I got across to the store.' Jonas had said he would look after the shop himself tonight, but Jonas also preached words like winds of change, and might change his mind about that.

'But you're not going,' Grandfather informed Maggie from the other side of the door, 'you're going to bed—Jonas's orders. I've made everything ready for you, Maggie, and as soon as you're snug under the rugs I'll bring in some soup.'

'Grandfather, I'm all right,' Maggie objected.

'Or tea,' Grandfather continued. He added: 'Jonas's orders.'

Jonas, Jonas! Maggie writhed.

'Tea!' she called.

She got lazily out of the bath and towelled herself desultorily. The episode certainly had affected her, she thought, she felt almost limp. She combed her fair hair and it clung tightly to her hand in small damp ringlets. It should be dried before she did what she had been ordered, go to bed, but Maggie suddenly found she had not the energy. She threw down the comb, wrapped herself up in an encompassing towel since she had not brought in a housecoat, then scuttled along the passage to her bedroom.

When she opened the door she stopped angrily. Jonas stood there.

'I thought you'd gone,' she told him.

'I had, but I came back. I'd forgotten to administer this.' He held out an open hand to her. 'No,' he said with amusement as involuntarily she twitched, 'it's not my palm across you as you well deserve, but a tranquilliser.' He nodded to a small capsule. 'I'm a strict believer in sedatives only on isolated occasions, but this is one of those occasions. Here's some water. Open your mouth.'

'No—I don't need it.' Maggie shut her mouth.

'Not at this moment, perhaps, but in a few hours you'll find you do.'

'I'll go to sleep.'

'And wake up from a bad dream. Don't waste my time, Maggie, open your mouth and swallow. If you don't I'll push this capsule between your lips and hold it there until you do.'

'You standing behind it?' Maggie burst out.

'That's the general idea,' he nodded.

'Then I've had enough of *that*, just hand me the thing.' She grabbed it and swallowed it without the water.

'See what you can do when you try,' he praised.

'And when I hate,' Maggie added.

Jonas decided to ignore that. He ordered: 'Don't stand around, get into bed.'

'I'm only in a towel,' Maggie said unwillingly.

'I'm not Blind Freddy,' he informed her, 'I'm well aware of that.'

Maggie looked down urgently, checked, then looked indignantly up again.

'It's a damp towel,' he pointed out, 'and dampness is revealing—over curves.'

'Perceptive Jonas, not Blind Freddy,' Maggie said contemptuously.

'A man doesn't need much perception in a case like this.' His eyes raked her. 'Here.' He had found her pyjamas and he tossed them across to her.

'After you go,' Maggie said haughtily.

He raised amused brows on her, his cobalt eyes

reminding her of his ministrations earlier that day, and Maggie felt even more choked than she had been with the choking earth. 'You——' she started to say.

'You're perfectly right,' he agreed blandly, 'but I did save you, didn't I? not only from death but a fate worse than death.' At her enquiring look he teased: 'I resisted you, Maggie. Tell me' . . . at the door now . . . 'would it have been worse than death?'

She took a deep, controlling breath. Then she said as coolly as she could: 'Tell Grandfather I'll have that tea now.'

From the hallway Jonas called: 'I've decided it's to be milk.'

Maggie wasted no time in getting into her pyjamas and climbing into bed. When the hot milk arrived the tranquilliser was already doing what was asked of it, and Maggie was only capable of establishing that it was Grandfather holding the beaker, not Brother Wolf. She accepted the warm drink and swallowed it. It must have been a strong sedative, she thought drowsily, lying back on the pillows, for she was drifting already.

In minutes she was asleep, and she slept for hours. She slept well into the next morning.

When Maggie opened her eyes there was a tray beside her. It could not have been there long, for the coffee still steamed. Gratefully Maggie reached out for it, and at once, hearing the chink of china, Grandfather appeared at the door.

'Awake?' he smiled.

'At last,' apologised Maggie.

'Don't you worry yourself over that, Maggie,

drink it down, then I'll bring some more, and some bacon and eggs.'

'I don't think I can——'

'Bacon and eggs,' said Grandfather. 'Jonas said.'

In which case, Maggie resigned herself after Grandfather had gone, it's bacon and eggs. She gritted her teeth.

She did justice to the meal when it came, though, for she had missed last night's dinner, and felt rather hollow. She was also relieved, though she would not admit it, when Grandfather announced that she was to stay in bed for the day—no doubt another 'Jonas said.' After she had given Grandfather back the depleted tray she slipped down into the sheets again—and once more she slept.

She came out of her oblivion mistily, so that it was some time before she could identify who it was standing beside her bed. Then, her vision clearing, she recognised Helen. Helen had actually found the courage, or whatever it was that had brought her here, to come up to the homestead!

Maggie opened her eyes fully and smiled a wide welcome. 'This is nice of you,' she said.

'It's not nice of *you*,' Helen responded with a touch of banter she never had used before, 'nearly killing yourself like you did.'

'It wasn't quite as bad as that,' Maggie said, 'but it was still bad enough.'

'Lucky for you that Jonas came along. When I flew in just now he was on the strip to tell me about it, then to ask me to call on you.'

'Jonas did that!' Considering how he had

scowled before, Maggie was amazed.

Helen did not answer, her eyes were roving around the room. Maggie watched her look beyond the room to the hall. 'It's been a long, long time . . .' Helen said almost indecipherably.

But Maggie caught the words. 'Since you've been here, Helen?' she asked. 'In the homestead?'

'Yes, Maggie.'

'You would be only a child then?'

'A little more than that; I was beginning to grow up, I was——'

'Verging on adolescent,' Maggie supplied.

'I was going to say nearly teenage,' Helen said.

'The same,' Maggie nodded. 'An in-between time.' She was thinking to herself, an emotional, sometimes difficult time.

Helen walked to the window, came back again. 'You know about it,' she said flatly.

'Only what Grandfather told me, and I don't think he really knew.' Maggie waited hopefully, but for nothing.

'No, I expect not,' said Helen, but she said no more.

'Helen, you asked me to go to Baden Wald with you.' Maggie broke a little silence.

Helen smiled. 'I didn't really, because I've never thought of it as that. It was the name my grandparents gave the house when they came here.'

'After their own house?' Maggie asked.

'Yes. At first in their newness they thought they could make it a second Baden Wald, but of course, when they experienced it they knew they never would.'

'Rust and ochre after green,' nodded Maggie. 'It

must have been hard.'

'They've never complained, and it's only lately that they've spoken of home.'

'Their home?'

'Yes. Maggie, I still want you to come and meet them. I even asked Jonas just now, and he said yes.'

'Jonas did?' Again Maggie was amazed. After his objections yesterday this really was a wind change. 'What exactly did Brother Wolf say?' she begged.

Helen widened her eyes at the name, and then, surprisingly for Helen, she giggled.

'Yes, that could be Jonas,' she agreed, 'but why Brother Wolf?'

'Brother to Timothy, who obviously isn't,' Maggie explained.

'No, Tim isn't.' Helen said in an indistinct voice, but Maggie still heard her.

A few more silent moments went by. Again Maggie broke the silence. 'So Jonas agreed to the invitation,' she marvelled.

'He did. You still want to come?'

'I want it very much.'

They talked lightly for a while, then Helen, glancing through the window, rose abruptly and announced that she must go. She added something about time passing . . . her need for good light. She seemed agitated.

'Very well, Cinderella,' Maggie tried to placate her.

'Why did you say that?' Helen was gathering her things together.

'You seemed suddenly very anxious to leave,' Maggie observed. 'Just like Cinderella at the stroke of twelve.'

'It's not twelve, and Cinderella had her Prince Charming.' By this time Helen had reached the door. Over her shoulder she called: 'I have none. Goodbye, Maggie.'

Maggie, about to ask her to stop a little longer, refrained. After all, it was a big thing, after eight years, for her to be here at all. So instead she called her own goodbyes as she listened to Helen's light steps down the hall. She certainly seemed in a hurry, Maggie mused. She wondered why.

Scarcely had the steps stopped than she heard more steps—stronger ones. She pulled the sheet up to her chin. It would be him again, she thought.

A moment later Tim came in. Maggie smiled at him; she always had a smile for Tim, and he for her. But this time, and actually the first time since she had met him, he had no smile in return. Even before he reached her bedside he was speaking angrily ... angrily for Tim ... at her. 'Never do that again, Maggie. Do you hear me? Never!'

'I hear you, Tim,' Maggie answered, 'but I don't know what you're talking about.'

'You know all right. The mine.' Tim was frowning at her.

'Oh, yes—it's taboo. Jonas has told me.'

'I told you, too, remember?'

'I remember, Tim, but I thought as the rock man here you might be pleased I took an interest.' Maggie looked keenly at him. What was this all about?

Tim had calmed down. 'Perhaps I am, Maggie, but I—we can't have you risking your life.

According to Jonas you could have been killed. Jonas was upset.'

'*I* was upset. I came out bedraggled.' But Maggie did not elaborate on that. She gave him a covert look. There was something odd here, she thought. She had a definite feeling that Tim's concern was not for her at all.

'I finished up perfectly all right,' she insisted, 'thanks to the arrival of your brother.'

'But why did he arrive? That's what I want to know,' Tim said moodily. 'If you hadn't gone there, Maggie, he wouldn't have followed you. See what you've done?'

'No, I don't see,' Maggie answered, puzzled, 'and Jonas didn't follow me, he was already there.'

'Jonas was? But why?'

'Oh, for pity's sake, Tim, how can I tell? I simply don't know what you're talking about. I don't understand you at all.' The frustration in Maggie's voice must have reached Tim, for he moved sensitively away from the bedside. He crossed over to the window to stare out, and, leaning up, Maggie saw he was watching the sky into which a small plane was ascending. It was Helen's little Cessna, and she silently observed Tim's gaze following it.

Still at the window, his voice muffled because his back was turned to her, Maggie heard Tim groan more than speak.

'How can you hope to understand me, Maggie,' he said, 'when I can't understand Tim Renwick myself?'

The evening brought Maggie's third visitor. Jonas returned to the sickroom, sauntering in and throwing his wide-brimmed paddock hat so expertly across that it landed on the bed.

'I learned that as a kid,' he boasted.

Maggie could think of several pertinent comments, but she forbore. Instead she waited for his next words.

'You seem fighting fit,' he observed. 'You can get up tomorrow.' As an afterthought he asked: 'How do you feel, Maggie?'

'As well as I must appear for *the doctor* to discharge me,' Maggie said coldly.

'You have the wrong man,' he drawled lazily. 'I'm the guy who was on the scene before the doctor. Remember?' He gave a downward grin, and Maggie followed his trend and tightened her lips.

But Jonas took no notice. 'Yes, you're fine,' he judged. 'No, that's not the word. You're beautiful.'

'The winds of change indeed,' Maggie marvelled. 'Before I definitely was not, you even went out of your way to tell me.'

'Not what?' he questioned.

'Not pretty.'

'You're still not,' he agreed, 'but you're beautiful.' He came nearer to the bed, apparently to retrieve the hat, but somehow Maggie could not accept his closer approach as just that. Instinctively she sank deeper under the rugs, and he grinned.

'Regular little mollusc, aren't you?' He said it lightly yet intentionally. 'You creep into your shell at a finger touch.' He extended a long brown finger, and Maggie shrank further down. In the muffling cover of the blankets she heard his low laugh.

'I'm not going to touch you, snail,' he assured her, and withdrew the finger. He sat down on the bed. She could feel the burn of his body even through the rugs into which she had burrowed, and she felt burned herself. 'So,' he observed, 'you've had a caller.'

'Two,' Maggie said. 'Helen and your brother.'

'We'll leave Tim out of it, I can manage him.'

'But not Helen?' Maggie asked.

'I never see her long enough to try myself out.'

'You saw her today,' Maggie reminded him.

'That's true, and she asked me could you go across to the de Merrils. I said yes. At the least, I decided, it would be a chance for you to learn something about her.'

'What?' disbelieved Maggie.

'You heard me,' he said impatiently. 'You could learn something about Helen.'

'And what would you expect me to learn?' Maggie's voice was shaken.

'That would be up to you. You could see her in her own surroundings, see those who surround her. After that you could report back to me.'

'Report—What are you asking me? What is this?' Maggie burst out indignantly.

'I'm asking you to look and listen and then tell me what you think of it all, how you consider I should handle it.'

'But this is quite abominable! Helen is my friend. Besides, I was never signed up as a spy.'

'Not a spy, you ninny, more a disinterested onlooker who will pass on her impressions to an interested one.'

'You?'

'Yes.'

'Then why don't you go and observe for yourself? You said you'd been asked.'

'But not socially invited as you've been,' he returned.

Maggie waited for him to explain, but when he did not she told him emphatically that she would not go.

'You will, though,' he corrected, 'and as soon as tomorrow morning. I've already rung Baden Wald.'

'You ride roughshod over everybody. Even if I did go ... though I won't ... I would never do those things.'

'What things?' he asked her.

'Spying. Snooping.'

'Why not, when you're an expert in them?'

Maggie did not answer that, and after a while Jonas got to his feet and walked up and down the room.

At last he came back and sat on the bed again.

'You're going to do it, Maggie,' he told her, 'because it's become important.'

'Important?' Maggie asked.

'For us.'

'Us——?' She stared at him.

'Just do it,' he ordered, and with that he left.

Important for us. What had he meant by that? Maggie puzzled over it for a long time after Jonas had gone. The man was mad as well as objectionable, she concluded; the sooner she got away from Phineas the better, and since even a short absence would be a relief she decided she would not fight Jonas after all, but go to the de Merrils as planned.

She awakened fresh and alert the next morning,
determined to make the day a day of discovery,
but not of Helen, or whoever it was affecting the
wolf, but something for her alone: a bolthole from
Phineas Acres. She would not stand it here much
longer.

She showered, breakfasted, then the moment she
heard the whirr of the Cessna she was on the field
waiting for Helen to taxi up to her.

'You can fly me *anywhere*, Helen.' They were
Maggie's first words as she climbed up. 'So long as
it's away from here.'

Helen laughed; she was in high spirits, her
cheeks pink as carnations, her eyes large and
eager.

'It couldn't be that bad, Maggie,' she said.

'It's worse. That man—that utterly impossible
man! The trouble is I don't know what he's talking
about when he says the things he does.'

Helen stopped touching her controls for a
moment to turn and look at Maggie. But all she
said was: 'I expect not. Fasten your belt.'

As Maggie did so, she began taxiing down the
paddock, then smoothly, very commendably, she
found wings.

A small craft was delightful, Maggie thought as
she looked over and out, much better than the
windows of larger planes which only framed
tatters of high cloud and an endless dome of sky.
This way the earth seemed to join with the
heavens, you did not feel disconnected, and you
had a view of everything, even though in this
instance everything was nothing, even no outcrop
of rock or dried-up river as at Phineas, no derelict
mine, only brown terrain with barely a tree as far

as you could see, and on the terrain the shadow of
the Cessna travelling with them.

'How do you find your way?' Maggie asked
Helen.

'I couldn't fail to find it,' Helen smiled back. 'I
turn right at the second cloud.'

'There aren't any clouds today,' Maggie pointed
out.

'There aren't any ever, there's only blue
and more blue. That's why all the properties
failed.'

'I can't imagine it was ever any different,'
Maggie said. She was remembering what she
had been told about the fertility of past
years.

'It's true, though,' Helen confirmed, 'it was a
long time ago, but it was rich and giving. The
Reptile River fed a large district. But then the
flow stopped, and to make it worse the rains
did, too.'

Maggie nodded, looking down again on the
ochre scene. 'I still can't see how you find your
way,' she said.

'I suppose you can't, but it's as clear to me as a
marked road. It should be, because I've done it
often enough.'

'Don't you ever go in another direction?'
Maggie asked.

'What would be the use? There's no other
station to go to for hundreds, not a hundred,
miles. No' . . . a pause . . . 'in every way it had to
be Phineas Acres.'

'In every way, Helen?' Maggie picked up.
Jonas was right, she thought with shame, I *am* a
snooper.

'In every way,' Helen said again.

They flew in silence for a while, Maggie no longer looking over and out, looking instead at Helen.

At last, aware of Maggie's gaze, Helen looked back at her.

'I love them, you see, and I love——' She never finished it. She indicated, rather with relief, thought Maggie, a distant cluster of buildings looming up, purplish from this distance, but quickly becoming definite.

'Is it your homestead?' Maggie asked.

'It's our home. I don't think homestead has come into it for many years. My grandfather did try to run it for a while, but he never understood it, never could face the dryness of it, the difference of it. He came from cool mountains, and this was dry desert, it was not his place, nor ever could be. But he still tried, and Grandmother with him, for me. In the end they just maintained it all—no crops, no stocks, just the home and what's around it. There are two men, one for the fields, one to service my father's plane.'

'The grandparents are not nervous about you flying?'

'Their son flew, so it was accepted that his daughter flew, too. No, Maggie, they're proud. Proud acceptance has always been their keynote . . . until now.'

'Until now?' Maggie probed again.

This time Helen did not reply.

Soon afterwards she told Maggie she was going to put down, and at once she did so very efficiently, even taxiing almost up to the usual wide verandah. In minutes the two girls were climbing shallow steps into a typical colonial farmhouse, but once beyond the entrance the Australian likeness stopped, and Maggie stepped a hundred years back and thousands of miles away.

She stood at the threshold and stared.

'Baden Wald.' It was Helen by Maggie's side. She took Maggie's hand and they went in.

The deeply glowing colours after the brash Australian lightness fascinated Maggie. She could hardly believe the world she had suddenly stepped into. Mahogany and red plush met her gaze, lavish chandeliers dripped golden brilliance, necessary since all the curtains were drawn against the western heat.

'Grandparents, this is Margaret,' Helen introduced her.

Maggie advanced further into the lovely old room. She almost felt that she should bow. But for all the European formality that followed she enjoyed herself.

The two old people brought back a past graciousness that warmed her; she found herself forgetting the unreal circumstances and drinking in every minute.

She sipped tea from exquisite china; respected the little niceties and courtesies her own generation seemed to have forgotten; she leaned back and relaxed; she felt wholly happy. For a while.

It all changed when Helen went out to replenish the teapot. Immediately the talk took on a different theme. It was still quiet, still gentle, still polite, but it was now intent as well. Instinctively Maggie stopped relaxing and sat up.

'We are honoured that you have come to Baden Wald with our granddaughter, Margaret.' The de Merrils shared this equally in rather laboured English. 'We are pleased Helen has found a friend. She must find us very dull company, must have found it so these many years, but please to understand she is all we have now—our son and his wife were——'

'Yes,' Maggie said sympathetically, 'I have been told.'

They nodded sadly and waited a moment. Then they began again.

'No doubt, being young yourself, you are thinking that we should have loosened our hold of Helen, perhaps sent her away to a school, at least done something more in keeping with her youth, something forward, not backward, but the disaster was very real to her, so catastrophic we could not take the risk of not being constantly near to her. At the time the doctor spoke of this, and we followed his advice.'

Maggie nodded. It was almost the same story as with Tim, she thought, only even more traumatic, for Grandfather was years away from a de Merril. What had happened to these two children, and why had it not happened to Jonas? Even if Jonas had 'slept' but they had not, it seemed an over-long reaction.

'Wouldn't it have been easier for you had you taken Helen to your own home, to the real Baden Wald?' she asked tactfully.

'No,' they both replied. 'No, that would have been a wrong thing, Margaret. Our son had become Australian, so it followed that his daughter must be, too. We accepted that at once.

It was always thus in our own country, you see, as father, as child. There was no hesitation in us to leave our home and cross the world for Helen. It was a wrench, but it had to be.'

Maggie nodded, very touched if a little puzzled.

'Unfortunately,' Mr de Merril was saying, 'it was a strange place to farm, so much different from home. I soon found I had not the skill.'

'It's a hard land,' Maggie murmured.

'Yet still Helen's land,' they both insisted. 'Her father came to it, married in it, Helen was born in it. So it had to be here, not there—we recognised that. We practised it. But we were younger then, and now . . .'

'And now at last you want to go back?' Maggie said intuitively.

The old lady gave her an eager look, but her husband gently restrained her.

'We are very old, Margaret,' he said, 'long past autumn, well into winter, and if we would return in the end it would fulfil a dear dear wish. All our friends are there. Our hearts are there. But it must not be like that for Helen. She is young, she is of this world. Our old shades are not for her. Perhaps we realise now that we should have foreseen this, have supplied her with more company, more opportunity, but what company and opportunity was there out here?' Before Maggie could speak the old man spread his fine hands. 'That is why——' he said.

'Yes?' Maggie asked, suddenly alerted. She noted a new firm look on the old lips.

'That is why the family who destroyed Helen's

parents, Helen's right to a proper life, must remedy what they have done. You look shocked, Margaret, but isn't it so?'

Maggie *was* shocked. For a while she was even speechless. But at last she said: 'It sounds rather like a tooth for a tooth. I doubt if we could ever look at it like that.'

'It is still the only way,' the old lady came in. 'Then why not? She is a very lovely girl.'

'She's a beautiful girl,' Maggie agreed, still feeling none of it was happening. 'But does she want that?'

'I do want it.' It was Helen standing at the door, the replenished pot in her hand. 'I want to marry him, Maggie. My grandparents are not coercing me—I, too, want it. That's why I've gone over every day. That is why I must continue to go.'

She came and put the teapot down, then looked almost challengingly at Maggie, but Maggie could see that her mouth was trembling.

'I love him,' she said simply. 'Why can't he love me? And why doesn't he ask?'

CHAPTER TEN

IT was a rather silent flight back to Phineas Acres.

After Helen's shock announcement . . . a shock to Maggie . . . nothing else had been said on the subject during the remainder of the girls' stay in

Baden Wald. The old people had returned to their polite conversation, more tea had been poured, and presently Helen had looked at the clock and announced that it was time to leave.

There were courteous goodbyes, then Maggie was climbing into the Cessna beside Helen. The girl made a similar smooth take-off as she had earlier from the Acres strip. Then, apart from the sound of flight, there had been quiet.

After a while the silence between herself and Helen depressed Maggie.

'Make sure,' she joked to the pilot, 'to turn at the second cloud.'

But Helen's smile back was a bare flicker. 'There are no clouds,' she pointed out.

'There is one big one,' Maggie dared. 'Can you tell me about it, Helen?'

'No.' Helen shook her head.

'Could you tell someone else, then? Could you tell—say, Jonas?'

'Jonas knows,' Helen said quietly. 'Please, Maggie, leave me alone.'

After that Maggie had not tried again. She had stared out at the ochre scene, seeing nothing. Jonas knows, Helen had just said, meaning, of course, that when Helen had stood at a doorway and blurted 'I love him' she had meant—Well, Maggie demanded impatiently, what else did I think?

It had been Jonas, she reminded herself, who had cleared the Phineas paddock in order to assure Helen's safety. It was Jonas who had met Helen yesterday and who had arranged for today. Looking back, it had always been Jonas. But why Jonas's web of deceit? Why his order that she, Maggie, spied on Helen, that she looked and listened, then reported back to him, told him how he should 'handle it'? Why Jonas's pretence of hating women when all the time there was a Helen de Merril? Why all these years of delay? Why most of all, and Maggie felt embarrassment flooding through her, a man's arms around another woman, around Maggie Wentworth, holding her as she had never been held before in all her life. A man's hard lips on hers. There was only one answer, Maggie decided. Diversion. It was apparent there was something not quite ready yet between Helen and Jonas, Maggie did not know what it was, but she was aware it was there, so while it came to fruition Jonas had filled in his time with someone else. With her. One thing, she knew now whom Jonas had meant when he had said, 'It has become important for us.' She had puzzled over 'us'. Now she was not puzzled. It was Jonas and Helen.

She jerked back to the present as suddenly the Cessna engine took on a different beat. She saw that Helen was losing height, that she was preparing to put down. Looking *and seeing* this time, Maggie found she was home.

'I won't get out, Maggie,' Helen told her, 'I have to watch the light. As soon as you're clear, I'll keep going.'

'Yes, Helen. Thank you, Helen. Goodbye, Helen,' Maggie said automatically as she climbed down from the plane.

Even before the Cessna was in the sky Maggie was racing to the homestead. She knew that at some time she would have to face Jonas, answer

... or evade ... his questions, but she felt she must have time to think about it first, prepare those answers or evasions.

That was what she planned, but it was not to be. Adroitly avoiding the office, or so she thought, she found suddenly Jonas was there in front of her.

'I heard the plane,' he said. 'Also your running steps. Except you're running in the wrong direction, Maggie. It's this way to the office.' He began veering her in the opposite direction.

'Not now,' she attempted. 'I mean, I have to get home for dinner. I mean, Grandfather is expecting me.'

'Not for another hour at least. It's still that and more to your normal knock-off time. Anyway, why the violent hurry? Surely you're not as hungry as all that? Surely the de Merrils fed you?'

'Certainly they did. They were very kind. But——'

'But you don't want to talk about it?' he asked.

'Not now,' she agreed.

'Then you're out of luck, we are going to talk about it.' He had led her to the office by now, opened the door and impelled her inside. There he sat her down, quite roughly, into the nearest chair.

'Begin,' he ordered.

'Begin what?' Maggie dared. 'I told you I was doing no spying, remember?'

'And I didn't hear you, remember? Now stop wasting my time and give me your impressions of today—and don't say you had no impressions, because I damn well know you had, a whole heap of impressions, by the way you were avoiding me just now.'

'But I didn't avoid you,' Maggie reminded him sourly.

'No—I copped you first. All right, shoot.'

'Shoot who?' Maggie said hopefully, hoping the hope sank in. At once Jonas leaned across and took her arm and held it with hard fingers.

'You can start with the plane trip,' he said. 'Was it comfortable? No squeamishness? Helen is a good pilot?'

'Yes, yes, and yes,' answered Maggie insolently, but she flinched as his entrapping fingers pressed her flesh.

'I'm not amusing myself, Maggie,' he warned. 'Not now.'

'Did you before?' she retorted.

'Before?' He pretended to think about it. 'Yes, I expect I did. What about you? Was it amusement, too? Even a kind of enjoyment?'

Maggie disengaged herself from him, rubbing the reddened skin where his fingers had bitten in. 'What is it you need of me?' she asked. 'I mean' ... at his rising brows ... 'what do you want to know?'

'Every damn thing about today,' he replied. 'Why the grandparents let that girl fly over here. What they're after. Why the whole unbelievable, farcical situation?'

'But you already know,' Maggie said.

'Perhaps, but I want to hear *you* say it, Miss Wentworth.'

'Then,' Maggie answered coldly, 'they let her fly over here because they are old and growing anxious for themselves as well as Helen. They are concerned with Helen's future. They believe, since the Renwicks did it all, then the Renwicks must be responsible. They think—well, they think——'

'Go on,' he said implacably.

'That Helen should——' Maggie stammered.

'Yes?'

'Marry here.' It was out at last.

A few moments went by. With luck he would stop his examining, Maggie hoped.

But he didn't. 'And Helen?' he asked. 'What about her?' His question came quite unsympathetically, typical of this man, Maggie thought. In that moment she knew she would not tell him. Not ever. Helen was far too good for him. He would only sneer at a report of a female standing at a door and saying 'I love him.'

'Well?' he prompted impatiently. 'What about Helen?'

'How would I know?' Maggie heard herself answer.

'She gave no indication how she felt?' he asked again.

'No.'

'None at all?'

'None at all. Why?'

There was quite a lengthy silence, then: 'So it was a wasted day, wasn't it?' Jonas said it quite carelessly, as though it didn't matter at all. 'Tomorrow,' he shrugged, 'seeing you were fit enough to take an air jaunt today, you can return to toil. Incidentally, while you were off sick some new guests came in.'

Maggie was surprised. 'Would there be room for them?' she asked.

'The old package group have left, laden down with the rot they've prospected, also, let's hope, some of the souvenirs you were expected to sell, but mostly didn't, by the look of the shelves. See to it you do better with this batch. You can go now,' he added. 'Grandfather will have the meal on. You can also skip the store tonight, start again in the morning.' Without even a nod Jonas went to the door, opened it and left.

After a minute Maggie left herself.

She was glad later when Grandfather, after giving her an intuitive look, did not question her. After eating the evening meal she pleaded weariness, and went to bed.

But again not to sleep.

She lay wide-eyed until the small hours, going through the day's happenings, wondering about the Renwicks, Helen, Helen's grandparents. Thinking of all the things left unsaid, unexplained. From people she went to places. Baden Wald. Phineas. The old mine. The mine, her fuzzy mind kept turning over, what about it? Why do my thoughts keep returning to the mine?

But try though she did Maggie's brain still kept going round in circles, and only an hour before dawn did she manage to drop off. She knew, as was always the case with her, that her weariness would show, so she determined to try to avoid Brother Wolf, knowing he would notice at once, let her know one moment after. In his customary way.

She was lucky. When she reached the office there was a note on her typewriter.

'Your chores today are social. Settle in the newcomers and show them around. But only, mark you, in your prescribed area. Alert Tim as to what's expected of him in the afternoon.' After that came briefly: 'J.'

Maggie put the note down.

First she went across to the motel to greet the new arrivals. After that she invited them to join in an initial tour of inspection, which she was pleased they all did. She included in the examination the dry river, the bunkhouse, the specimen shop, other 'safe' things that Jonas could not frown over. She put everything into her guiding and felt she did well. Telling the tourists the opening time for the store each day, and, with Jonas in mind, the gem souvenirs they could buy if they were not lucky themselves, she left them to their own resources until their journey farther afield in the early afternoon with Tim. Just to be sure of Tim she went across to his lab to prompt him.

He promised he would not forget, and Maggie promised she would not let him. But she had to say it twice. This morning he seemed more inattentive then ever.

'Tim,' she said sharply, 'two o'clock! You're conducting the newcomers.'

'Yes, of course. Maggie——'

Something in his voice caught her attention.

'Yes, Tim?'

'There has been no plane fly in yet.'

'No, the batch arrived yesterday,' Maggie said.

'I don't mean the charter, I mean—the Cessna.'

'Cessna?' she queried.

'Helen's Cessna. Helen hasn't come today. When you left her yesterday was she all right?'

'Of course, Tim. I expect it was just a bit too much flying over again today.'

'Yet she always does it,' Tim said.

'Not twice in a short time,' Maggie reminded him.

He thought about that. 'I suppose you're right, but——'

'She's quite all right, Tim, I'm sure of that.'

Again he said: 'I suppose so.' He apologised: 'One thinks of accidents. They do happen.'

'One hasn't happened this time, and don't let anything happen with your memory this afternoon.'

He nodded, and Maggie went back to the office. But when she got there she found that she, too, was missing the now familiar sound of the Cessna. On an impulse she took up the phone and rang through to Baden Wald.

Helen's voice came over the wire.

'Helen, are you all right? It's Maggie.'

'Hullo, Maggie. Yes, I'm fine. And you?'

'You didn't come across.' Maggie skipped Helen's polite rejoinder.

'No, I didn't.'

'Why?'

A silence, then: 'Why do you think, Maggie? You know I made a fool of myself yesterday.'

'I don't know that at all, I only know I miss you, that I would very much like you here now. Please, Helen.'

There was no response.

'*Please*, Helen!'

'I'll see.' Helen's phone went down.

But the next day, and the next, she still did not come.

Maggie threw all her energy into her job. This

time she was resolved that Brother Wolf, however close he looked, would find nothing to complain about.

She conducted the wives everywhere until at last they complained laughingly that they would like to be let loose to prospect themselves now—their husbands were doing so, so why not they?

Maggie smilingly agreed, assuring them that she had not been deliberately occupying them to keep more gems for herself. As she said it she wondered, gems? Or sheep? Was Tim right? Or Jonas? Well, it was nothing to do with her, her only goal was escape, and as quickly and quietly as was humanly possible. She knew now she could not go on much longer, not under *his* direction. In readiness she even packed a bag. It was a small bag, it had to be, but leaving most of her possessions behind her did not cause any regrets. So long as she escaped.

Yet escaped actually from what? In spite of herself Maggie found that a hard question to answer. How could you escape from a place you had come to like quite a lot? From people you liked a lot? The tourists were amiable, Grandfather lovable, Tim a friend, the de Merrils charming. There was only *him*.

Yet even Jonas, in a reverse kind of way, at least was interesting. For all her determined *un*interest in him, Maggie still knew that she had failed. The fellow attracted her, evilly no doubt, but he still could not mean nothing to her. She knew she was always aware of him—too aware. Also Helen's 'I love him' had affected her more than she could have believed, or would ever admit. Why did she feel like this?

She was still musing over it all as she left the homestead to open up the trading post that evening, and her anger at her unwanted interest in Jonas must have shown clearly, for when Jonas unexpectedly joined her he commented at once.

'Temper, temper,' he chided. 'It flies like a flag from you. What happened today, then? Someone pose a question you couldn't answer?'

'I know now to refer the questions to you.' Maggie held on to her self-control with difficulty. Why, she was wondering, can't I ever be indifferent with this man?

'Not always,' he suggested, getting into step beside her to cross with her. 'By this time there must be quite a few queries you can answer yourself. As you open up the store and get ready for the thriving trade I trust you've coaxed back to the business, I'll try you out.' He took the key from Maggie and opened the door, but he did not leave it open for customers, instead he shut it behind them, shut it lightly but firmly.

Then he turned to Maggie and looked at her.

'Question one,' he began . . . then stopped.

'I'm waiting for you,' said Maggie after a few silent moments, and she said it as calmly as she could. For something had happened to her. Standing there in the dim interior, for the blinds had been drawn against the late afternoon heat, she was more conscious of this man than she had ever been with any man, anywhere.

Across the few feet between them his maleness almost accosted her. She could feel his body heat in the planned coolness of the store; it inflamed her.

'Are you?' His voice came rather huskily from the semi-light. He came a step nearer.

'Am I what?' Maggie pretended not to understand him.

'Waiting for me? You said you were waiting. *Are* you, Maggie?'

'Jonas?' she said a little tremblingly. She did not want to shiver like this, but all at once she could not control herself.

'Oh, Jonas, is it?' he pounced. 'Not Brother Wolf? That at least is a little better. Yet somehow ... right now ... I feel more like Brother Wolf than Jonas Renwick.' His blue eyes, wide lawless blue eyes at this moment, were riveting Maggie's own eyes, and suddenly she felt she could meet the gaze no longer, yet she still dared not look down. If she did, she knew, he might advance, and she wanted all her senses, all her saneness, to stop him from that. Stop him—for Helen.

For, and helplessly Maggie knew this, in spite of Helen, and what Helen had said, in spite of *everything*, she, Maggie Wentworth, wanted Jonas Renwick to come.

Come to her.

CHAPTER ELEVEN

I WANTED Jonas to take me in his arms—tightly, shutting everyone else out. I wanted Jonas to hold me there, keep me there, for ever.

Maggie kept turning this over in her mind as

she dealt unaided with the new intake. I wanted
Jonas ... wanted him. It always came back to
that.

She tried to concentrate on the customers, who
were more numerous tonight than previously.
They seemed pleased with this unexpectedly
adequate little shop in the middle of nowhere, and
they spent freely. Maggie hurried between them,
found things, accepted payment, but her mind
kept revolving around her sudden revelation, that
instinctive wanting in her of Jonas. That awareness
that though she did not like him, there was still a
wanting. What in pride's sake was wrong with her?
she thought.

In the finish Jonas had come no closer to her in
the unopened store. Over the short distance
between them he had looked levelly at her for an
unwavering minute, then, without any warning
that she would be coping alone, he had left. He
also had left the door half closed behind him, and
after a stunned moment, for she had expected him
to come but not known how she would react,
Maggie had admitted the first customer. Soon the
shop had been filled.

It was the same as on the Reef, she thought as
she parcelled purchases, no bunch of tourists was
exactly the same as the bunch before. This group
bought more extravagantly than the initial intake,
so at least Brother Wolf should be pleased about
that. By closing time the till was almost full,
and Maggie smiled the last customer away,
then tallied the takings. They were very satisfactory.

But not so satisfactory were her persistent
thoughts. How, she wondered in disgust, can I

feel attracted to someone I find unattractive, someone I dislike, someone who obviously dislikes me in return? Jonas has 'amused' himself with me, even boasted of it, but there has never been any feeling in him for me, not even much interest. It just happened that I was there. *And a woman.* For it finally came down to that, Maggie accepted: that for Jonas Renwick there had to be a woman. So much for a hater of them! she thought.

But there was going to be only one woman in the future for him, Maggie's mind ran on. In spite of Jonas's apparent offhandedness with Helen, Jonas still had said: 'It is important for us,' and Maggie knew now whom he had meant.

Well, it could not matter to her ... but the puzzle still remained with her that a strong man like Jonas could not solve whatever he had to solve on his own account and not ask her help. Also, that a strong man like Jonas should need a palliative, name of Maggie Wentworth, until his solution was reached. That a solution was necessary to him, for shouldn't love solve all? Nothing fitted and nothing fell in place, Maggie decided. On that unsatisfactory note she closed up and crossed to the homestead and bed.

Again the next day, and the following day, there was no Cessna, no Helen. Several times, when Jonas was not around, Maggie took up the phone to ring the de Merrils. Then she put it down again. Brother Wolf, she reminded herself, had a habit of suddenly appearing, and she did not want to be caught 'snooping' again, as it pleased Jonas to tag it. Also, what could she actually say to Helen? If Helen had decided not to come across to Phineas any more what could Maggie do?

Curiosity, however, eventually spurred her, and she did ring. But when a voice answered, and it was not Helen's, she became so unsure of herself that she could only murmur her name, and after that an apology to Mrs de Merril for not having thanked her earlier for her hospitality.

Mrs de Merril was polite ... were the de Merrils ever impolite? ... but a little surprised that Maggie had not given the message to their granddaughter. How could I do that when Helen was not here, and has not been here? Maggie thought. At that moment she heard the whirr of a little plane— Helen's Cessna. At last, she sighed, bidding goodbye to Mrs de Merril and replacing the phone. She listened for Helen's putting-down sound, but caught only a diminishing beat. She hurried to the door of the office to peer out. In the distance she could see the Cessna receding, then, as she watched, it turned and came back.

Almost at once Jonas strode along. 'What in Betsy,' he demanded furiously, 'is that female doing up there?' Helen was circling now.

'Perhaps she's practising,' Maggie said inadequately.

'Perhaps she's playing the fool,' he retorted.

'Why not?' Maggie said defiantly. 'You always go out of your way to show her she's not wanted here.'

'Well, I damn well don't want her up there, either, it's quite out of the question!'

'For yourself, the guests, or Helen?' Maggie enquired.

'All three,' Jonas swore. He turned his angry eyes from the sky to Maggie. 'What a question! You must be the most maddening woman I've ever had round me!'

'Have there been many?' Maggie asked impertinently.

'Too many, with you.' At the sound of the Cessna as it circled again Jonas ordered: 'Get in touch with that girl when you judge she's home again, ask her what the hell she thinks she's doing.'

'Shouldn't that be your job?' Maggie suggested.

'You mean as the boss,' he said.

'No, I meant as the——' As the one Helen is interested in, Maggie had meant, as the one Helen comes here for, as the one she *loves*. That other human unit in your importance double. But she did not say any of it, instead she told him: 'I've already rung, but the grandparents, not Helen, answered.' She paused. 'They believed she was over here.'

'Hell, she is over here.' Jonas looked up.

'You understood what I meant,' Maggie said coolly.

'Yes, I did. But for the life of me I can't understand her.' A quick suspicious glance at Maggie. 'Do you?'

'No,' lied Maggie ... for she did. She understood what Jonas for some reason was choosing not to understand. It was the fact that Helen loved him, and in love you had to be close.

'I'll ring again,' she said.

That night, while Grandfather was in his kitchen, she did, and this time Helen answered.

'Helen, you can't do what you're doing any longer,' Maggie began at once. 'There's been a protest.'

'So he noticed,' was all Helen's reply.

'Yes. Why did you? It's so silly to fly over but not put down as you have always done.'

'Keep your voice low, Maggie.' Helen's own voice came softly but urgently. 'I did put down, of course. I mean *they* think that.'

'Your——'

'Yes, Maggie. Please be quiet.'

'You mean,' persisted Maggie in a softer tone, 'your grandparents believe you've been here each day?'

'Yes.'

'Where were you, Helen?'

'The same as today. Up there somewhere making circles and filling in time. I had to think.'

'Think about what? You're not still worrying over what you said?'

'That I love him? No, Maggie, I'm not. I *do*, and I *said* it, so what would be the use? No, it's my two dear people, my grandparents. I've been watching them closely, and I've realised that I can't let them wait any longer. Maggie, I'm going to act.'

'Act, Helen?' queried Maggie.

'Do what I should have done long ago.'

'Which is?'

'Move right away from here,' Helen said.

Maggie considered that. 'But would it satisfy them? Would it send them home happy and reassured? Duty done?'

'Yes, it would, Maggie, and at once . . . if they were told I'd gone *there*.' Helen waited a few moments. 'Not for just a day, but every day—always.'

'Where is *there*?' Maggie waited falsely for Helen.

'Phineas—the Renwicks. What they've always wanted.'

'Wanted permanently, Helen.' Maggie looked at the girl.

'Yes, Maggie. And permanency is what they're going to hear, Maggie, and they'll be so happy, so relieved, I know they'll make their move at once. It's what they have waited for, but it never happened. I don't think now it ever will. But I'm not letting them know that.'

'What exactly will you do?' Maggie asked carefully. Already something was occurring to her, something that, through Helen, she might be able to achieve for herself.

'Soon I'll break the "happy" news, Maggie. I'll tell them I'm saying goodbye to them, and I'll tell them why.'

'After that?' Maggie prompted.

'After that I'll insist that they don't wait any longer, I shall remind them that time is passing, that when they leave I can leave—to Phineas, to be married. But of course, I won't be going to Phineas to be married but to The Alice—still unmarried.' Helen gave a high unnatural laugh. 'At Alice I shall sell the Cessna and take the first transport available to the city.'

'Which city, Helen?'

'Does it matter? Just so long as I can free them, free myself. I can't bear their estrangement and loneliness any longer. They're so old and they yearn for their own old world. They did everything for me, now it's my turn to do something for them.'

'If it can work. If they'll believe you.'

'They always have. Just wish me luck, Maggie.'

'You know I do, Helen. But there's something I have to ask you.' As Helen waited, Maggie begged: 'Take me with you.'

'Are you serious?' asked the other girl.

'Take me, too.'

There was a silence at the other end, then Helen said: 'No, I couldn't do that.'

'If you refuse,' Maggie said in an even lower voice, 'you would be leaving me—with Jonas.'

'Why not?' queried Helen.

'Why not?' Maggie echoed incredulously. But before she could say anything Helen had rung off.

Maggie tried to ring again, but the line did not respond. When she arrived at the office in the morning she tried once more. Again there was no answer ... deliberately, she guessed, and, seeing Jonas approaching, she put the phone down.

'I trust you've stopped that circling nonsense,' Jonas began at once. 'Did you ring the de Merrils?'

Many times, Maggie thought privately. Aloud she murmured: 'Yes.'

'You told Helen what I told you?' he demanded.

'Something of the sort,' she evaded.

Jonas looked at her suspiciously. 'What does that mean?' he asked.

'I gave her the message,' she replied.

He came and stood directly in front of her.

'I don't think I like your attitude this morning,' he informed her.

Irritated by him, by everything lately, Maggie retorted: 'I don't like you. That's why——'

'Yes?'

Maggie had been about to blurt, 'That's why I'm leaving here—I don't know how, but I am.' With it still trembling on her lips, she substituted: 'That's why I answer you back, Mr Renwick, even though I know one shouldn't answer a boss back.'

'So they taught you that, did they?' He said it almost lazily, his attention, Maggie saw, had wandered. His long brown forefinger had come forward to flick at her fair hair.

'Cream,' he mused. 'Like the waves at your Compass Bay. Is that why they employed you there? To match?'

'If it was, wouldn't you be employing a redhead?' Maggie nodded beyond the door to the tawny terrain.

'I prefer red hair,' Jonas drawled, 'but on this occasion I had to take what came.' He looked speculatively at her. 'So you never answered a boss back before?'

'No,' Maggie agreed.

He smiled. 'Then if nothing else I've started that.'

'Started what?'

'Revolt. But I'm not worried, I can handle revolt, even enjoy it. Like this.' Without any warning he drew Maggie to her feet, wrapped her in his arms, then compelled her face up to him. He waited a deliberate moment to let her know what he intended doing, then slowly ... very slowly ... giving her every opportunity to rebel, he kissed her. It was a kiss with nothing at all in it, and

Maggie, guessing the game he was playing, that game of revolt, stood apparently docile while it was going on. He wanted her to rebel so he could show her how he could handle her, but did it have to be in such a cool, nothing way as this?

Presently he shrugged and released her.

'You're not much to kiss, Miss Wentworth,' he told Maggie. 'At least not yet.'

'I never will be, for you,' she returned.

'For someone else, then? Do I know him?'

'Mr Renwick, can I go?' Maggie burst out.

'Go? Of course not. You're at work. Indeed, you've barely begun.' He looked at his watch. 'Why do you want to go? Where?'

'I want to go because of you, and I want to go anywhere that's away from you.' Maggie was still rankling under that nothing-at-all kiss. If he had had to kiss her, why at least hadn't he made the kiss what a kiss purported? Why wasn't he a man?

To her horror she heard herself saying so, and she flinched at his furious look.

'So you think I'm not a man?' he challenged. 'Do you want proof?'

'I'm sorry, I shouldn't have said that.' Nervously Maggie began to edge away.

To her surprise he permitted her to do so. He even laughed softly and uninterestedly as she did. Of all things he patted her head—paternally. 'Not to worry, little one,' he said, 'because I don't.'

. . . But will you, Maggie wondered, when you find Helen gone?

However, Jonas was not worrying at this moment, he was leaving the office, hat pulled over his eyes against the western glare, thumbs under the silver buckle of the belt holding up his cords. As soon as he was out of sight, Maggie left, too.

Taking a circuitous route in the direction of the garages, at last she reached the Phineas collection of tractors, cars, waggons and jeeps. At least I can *drive*, she was thinking, at least I can get *away*.

But someone else seemed to have a similar idea. As Maggie got there she saw Tim. He was standing considering a tough little four-wheel drive, looking thoughtful.

He wheeled round in surprise as Maggie came up.

'I trust we don't quarrel over the same one.' She made herself say it flippantly, for Tim looked anything but that. Instead he looked intent, something foreign to him, for though he was often abstracted, always dreaming, sometimes sad, only once did Maggie remember him intent. It had been that time she had gone to the mine, she mused, she had not known his reason then for his intensity, just as she did not know his reason for it now. She went to ask, but he spoke before Maggie could.

'Why are you here, Maggie?' he said.

'The same reason as you, Tim?' Maggie said back.

'I just happen to be here, there's no particular reason.'

He was being evasive, Maggie knew that; Tim was easy to read, not like Brother Wolf. She smiled her disbelief at him.

'No reason yet your serious look at this tough

little model? Admit it, Tim, you were wondering whether it could get you to—Where was it to get you?'

'Maggie, I just told you that——'

'That there was no particular reason.' Maggie decided to accept that. She did not believe him, but she would not press the matter. Tim was too nice, too likeable, too vulnerable for that.

'*I* have a reason,' she announced instead. 'The reason of escape.'

He showed no surprise. 'Escape from Phineas?' he asked.

'I like Phineas. No, escape from him.'

Tim did not question 'him', instead he looked very gravely at her. 'But you must get that idea out of your head,' he said.

'Leaving here?' Maggie questioned.

'Leaving here *this* way.' Tim nodded to the jeep. 'You wouldn't last an hour.'

'You're exaggerating.'

'I'm not. Even I, who live here, would give it a considering look.'

'So you *were* thinking in the same strain as I was,' Maggie pounced.

'No, of course not. Don't jump to conclusions. The transport has to be checked regularly, and I . . .' Tim stopped, then: 'Yes, Maggie, perhaps I was.' He added at once: 'But it was just a passing thought.'

'Well, mine wasn't passing, Tim, and it hasn't passed. You see, I can't stay here any longer. I can't wait for the charter. The way it comes in filled and goes out filled I could be stuck here for months, and I couldn't bear months. So' . . . Maggie took a deep breath . . . 'I'm going to borrow one of these things and get out by myself.'

'No, Maggie,' Tim said adamantly. He shook his head.

'I believe you're meaning you would report me?' Maggie demanded.

'If you made me,' he regretted. 'I would hate doing it, but if I didn't it might well be the end of you.'

'You're exaggerating,' Maggie said again. 'I only want to go a hundred miles.'

Tim looked at her sharply at that. 'There's only one place as near as a hundred miles.'

She nodded. 'It's *that* place,' she said.

'Baden Wald?'

'The de Merrils', yes.'

'But why there?' There was something in Tim's voice now that made Maggie look quickly at *him*.

'Didn't you just say it was the only place as near as a hundred miles?' she reminded him.

'Yes, it is ... but, Maggie, what are you planning? There *is* a plan, I think.'

'Yes, Tim, I plan to go to Baden Wald, and then leave with Helen.'

Now Tim stepped right up to her. 'With Helen!' he exclaimed.

'Yes.'

'Is Helen going?' A pause. 'Is she leaving?'

Maggie waited, then she said: 'Yes, she's leaving.' If Helen had wanted it kept strictly secret she should have told her.

'Helen ... leaving...' Tim said it in an odd kind of voice.

A long moment went by. It seemed to Maggie to go on for ever.

Tim broke it, but not as Maggie had expected. He left Helen, and returned to what Maggie had told him she would do.

He said quietly and intensely: 'Every one of those hundred miles you're considering will be either sand, gibber or outcrop, every inch of each mile will be hopeless camouflage. There's no marked road, only a barely discernible track, a track that could baffle an expert . . . and has. Even old hands have been known to give up, sometimes too late. You can't play around with this far west.'

'You're painting a frightening picture, Tim,' she said worriedly.

'I'm trying to. I want you to know that if you have any ideas of creeping away when no one is watching, then you can feasibly say goodbye for ever. It has happened.'

'No loss,' Maggie shrugged with mock bravado, 'perhaps, after him, my gain.'

Again Tim did not question 'him'. He was too absorbed. Instead he said: 'Then there are the others.'

'What others?'

'The rescue parties who would feel obliged to search for you.'

That sobered her. She tried to find words to answer him, but none came. Tim took advantage of her silence.

'You see, they would search, Maggie, it's a western code, and possibly some of them would search too far.' He let that sink in. 'So don't do it, except under supervision.' The moment he had said that he looked away quickly. He was transparent, Maggie thought, she could read him at once.

'*You*, Tim?' she asked. '*Your* supervision?'

'No,' he said. He repeated anxiously: 'No. No, I couldn't.'

'You mean you would be unable to?' she pretended to interpret.

'I would be able to, Jonas and I know this place like the backs of our hands, but——'

'But you won't?'

'No, Maggie, I won't.'

'Then, Tim, short of you stopping me physically, which I know *you* would never do, I'm still going. I have to. Can't you understand?'

'No, I can't, but I do hear what you're saying, and I'm begging you—*begging* you, Maggie, to have second thoughts.'

'I'm still going to Baden Wald, and after that with Helen.'

'With Helen.' Again Tim said that. 'Why is she leaving? Did she say?'

'She's at the end of everything, as I am,' Maggie said quietly. 'Getting out is the only way.'

'But what did she *say*?'

'Her grandparents came into it; they want to go home, but they won't until——' Maggie left that unfinished.

'I asked you, Maggie,' Tim repeated, 'what did Helen *say*?'

She looked at him. For a moment she felt like telling him about Helen standing at a door and calling, 'I love him.' But what interest would that be to Tim?

'Nothing really,' she said instead. 'I'm as knowledgeable about everything out here as I was when I first came to the place. I know nothing at all, and nobody tells me.'

'Yet you would leave still not knowing,' Tim asked.

'I told you,' Maggie returned bluntly, 'I'm leaving with Helen.' She did not add that Helen did not know that yet. She waited a moment, then begged: 'Tim, take me.'

'I couldn't.'

'Why couldn't you?'

'Because——' he turned away from her. He even walked away, then he wheeled back again. He had lost his uncertainty, and looked intent again. 'Though perhaps it could be an idea,' he said. 'Perhaps *you* would be a good idea.'

'A good idea?' Maggie was puzzled.

'It's been so long since we've spoken . . . it could be awkward . . .'

'Awkward?' she queried.

'Perhaps it would help if *you* were there, too.'

Maggie could not follow him, but she wasted no time pushing an advantage. 'You will take me, then?'

'I didn't say so. Anyway, Jonas wouldn't permit it.'

'Your brother needn't know. I mean, Tim, he's not in the office that much to notice, he would only think I was out with the guests—after all, he tells me to do things like that.'

'No,' Tim said again. 'What would Jonas say when I came back alone?'

'You wouldn't be alone,' Maggie lied. 'I only want to *tell* Helen at this juncture. After that it would be nothing to do with you.' She willed her voice not to falter, for she had no intention, once she left Phineas, of ever returning again.

Tim was still looking uncertain, murmuring his

uncertainties aloud, but Maggie judged that if she talked long enough and convincingly enough she could persuade him. For some reason she could not understand he kept coming back to Maggie being an advantage, and Maggie took advantage of that.

Eventually he gave in.

'We'll leave early in the morning,' he said. 'What about Grandfather? Will he raise an alarm if you're not there for breakfast?'

'I'll fix that,' Maggie assured him. Already in her mind she *had* fixed it . . . an emptied cup laid out on the table, a spoon beside it, a hurried note saying she was starting early today so had fixed her meal herself. A casual, See you later.

'Then at daybreak,' Tim said. 'I'll bring some biscuits in case we're hungry. Not a word, Maggie.'

'Not a word,' Maggie assured him.

She went back to the office and put so much work into the rest of the day that Jonas, calling in and seeing her results waiting his attention on his desk, raised a brow and drawled: 'Anyone would think you won't be appearing here any more.'

As he did not make a question of it, Maggie pretended she had not heard.

Work finished, she went over to the homestead and had her usual dinner with Grandfather, taking care not to mention tomorrow's early rising. She knew if she did Grandfather would be up, too, to make sure she was suitably nourished, and he would ask questions she could not answer.

Her determination trembled a little as she

wished him goodnight. She had come to love the
old man, and, who knew, this might be her last
contact with him. He was growing older and she
would be far away, too far to come to him. Almost
as though Grandfather felt something, too, he
paused a moment.

Then, with a gruff 'Sleep well, Maggie,' he went
down the hall.

Maggie showered so as to be as quick as
possible tomorrow, went straight to bed pretending
she was a dead log, an old, sometimes successful
device, and, to her surprise the next morning,
slept.

It was piccaninny daylight when she tiptoed
from the homestead, but by the time she reached
the garages the grey was dissolving into pearly
white.

Tim, waiting, drew her attention to some
scavenging dingoes on the fringe of the project.
One had knocked over a bucket, and as Maggie
crossed to right it, the dingo raced fleetly away
from her. They were nervous animals.

She climbed into the stout little jeep that Tim
had selected, and with a minimum of noise he set
out in a direction he told her was north-west.

'Now where,' he smiled at Maggie, 'is your
road?'

He was right. The first indentations petered out
almost within yards, and from then on Maggie
could not work out which track from the scores of
apparent tracks Tim would follow. She amused
herself trying to discover which one she would
have selected, but was wrong so often she gave up,
and instead looked around her.

At first it was Phineas Acres all over again, flat,

red, ochre yellow. Then there was a sudden
surprise section of distant lupin-blue hills, a herd
of buffalo on them, headed, Tim told her, by
buffalo hunters. The hunters were too indistinct to
see, though, and Maggie had to content herself
with some brumby camels, and, to her joy, for
they were very pretty, a passing flock of pink and
grey galahs.

Some miles out Tim turned unerringly off the
track he was following to a wurlie he knew.
Maggie had learned by this time that a wurlie was
a watering hole, but she had not anticipated such a
pretty setting. It was blue from the sky, not ochre
like everything else out here, and dragonflies flew
over it, gnats settled, and, though she saw no sign
of him, a frog croaked.

'Is it in use?' she asked, cupping her hands in the
cool water. She took a drink.

Tim had taken out the biscuits he had brought
along. 'It is now,' he said. 'Yes, Maggie, it is in
use.' He pointed to some dingo pads, some snake
trails.

It was pleasant there, but, Tim wisely warned,
no one knew for certain how a journey would
turn out, soft sand could slow you up, a patch
of gibber could puncture you, so they did not
dally. They were soon back on the invisible track
again, and an hour later the de Merrils' house
was in sight.

At once the atmosphere between then, pleasant,
relaxed, anticipatory, altered. Almost as though he
was a balloon and someone suddenly had deflated
him, Tim stopped the jeep and asked helplessly:
'Maggie, what do we do now?'

She turned and looked at him. 'Do? What we

came to do, of course. We see Helen.'

'Helen——' echoed Tim. Then he said: 'No. No, I can't.'

'But this is ridiculous,' Maggie protested. She repeated: 'It's what we came for.'

'No, I can't. It's been too long. Far too long,' Tim said in a low, tight voice, a voice that compelled Maggie's sympathy in spite of her irritation. She looked at him. He was deathly pale.

'What is it, Tim?' she asked, concerned.

'Maggie, I'm going back. I was a fool to come. I'm sorry, Maggie.'

'But, Tim——'

'We'll both go back,' Tim said.

'*I* am not going back, and by the look of you, you'd better wait as well. What's wrong, Tim? There must be something.'

'There's nothing,' he said stubbornly. 'I just can't be here, that's all.'

'But, unless I go with you, you can't return. You're in no condition to return.' Maggie knew she was right, all at once Tim was looking ghastly. 'At least,' she tried to coax, 'come to the outskirts. I'll go in and get something for you, something restoring. You *must*, Tim.'

'No,' Tim said quite desperately.

In the end Maggie snatched the key from the ignition. At least he would be unable to get anywhere while she ran over to the house. Tim watched her do it and said nothing. He seemed almost inert.

'I won't be long, Tim,' Maggie said bitterly, not bitter against him but bitter against the way fate was treating her. How could she *not* return now with Tim?

She started off to Baden Wald. Halfway there she was relieved to see a small car coming out to meet her. Helen drove it.

'I saw you,' said Helen when she reached Maggie. 'Wasn't there . . . isn't there someone else with you?' Her voice stopped sharply, and Maggie saw she was looking at the jeep.

'Yes, it's Tim, Helen. He's not well. Can you give me something for him?'

There was no reply.

'Helen, can you give me something for him?' Maggie tried again.

'Why did he come?' said Helen in an unreal voice.

'To bring me. Helen, can you—*Helen*——' For Helen had turned her eyes from the jeep to look at Maggie, and Maggie saw she was crying.

'There's a flask of tea here, some sandwiches, I was taking them out to the men. I can get more.' Helen handed them to Maggie and Maggie took them gladly.

'Helen, I'm still leaving with you,' she said. 'I brought my bag today, I was going to stop, but——'

'But you can't.' Helen looked to the jeep again. 'I won't go without you, Maggie. I told you I wouldn't take you, but I will—if you go back with Tim. Take him home. Take him carefully. Take him safely.' The tears were still in Helen's eyes. 'Will you do it?' she begged.

'Will you do it for me?' Maggie answered.

'I promise I'll take you when I leave. I promise it, Maggie. I'm sorry you've had all this worry. It's just—just——' Helen searched vainly for words.

'It's been just too long?' Maggie asked, recalling what Tim had said.

Helen nodded.

Maggie turned and went back to the jeep. She did not know whether Helen was watching her, for she did not turn round to look. She was wondering how Jonas would have reacted to all this, and involuntarily she shivered. She need not have been nervous, though, for it was a long time before Jonas did any considering.

After coaxing the hot tea into Tim, and one of the sandwiches, they set off again, Maggie keeping a keen eye on the brightness of the day, for she was driving, perforce doing it slowly and carefully, and she did not want to run out of light.

They had been on the invisible track, Tim instructing Maggie, less than an hour when the jeep suddenly spluttered, then stopped.

'I do believe we're dry,' Maggie exclaimed, appalled. She looked enquiringly at Tim.

He tried to look back at her, but couldn't. A few moments went past before he spoke.

'I knew there was some in last night, but not enough. I intended to fill her right up this morning, but I forgot. My God, can I ever do anything right?'

He put his head in his hands and kept it there. 'Have I ever done anything right,' he muttered, 'since then?'

Hours after, darkness all round them, Maggie puzzled over those words.

CHAPTER TWELVE

SLOWLY but eventually Maggie prompted Tim out of his depression. She persuaded him to find their predicament not so disturbing as exasperating. How, she asked, could they have fallen for the timeworn trap of running out of fuel? . . . she was careful to include herself in the blame . . . how could they have been such fools?

At last Tim came to see it her way: a rueful matter but not a catastrophic one. They even managed to grin at each other.

Some ringnecked parrots, bright in the still brazen sunlight, encouraged them, and soon Tim was drawing Maggie's attention to a wedge-tailed eagle, brilliantly accentuated by the copper distance and his sheer height. In the end all she could do was speak wistfully of Grandfather preparing a wonderful meal, while Tim remembered guiltily that he had had a tour to guide. But these were all their worries until the first touch of dusk took them unawares.

Maggie first realised night was falling when she could see Tim no longer.

'Tim,' she gasped, 'it's dark!'

'Yes,' Tim agreed. 'It looks as though we'll be here until morning, Maggie, because no one tackles the desert this late. We may as well sit back and relax and wait for our rescue.'

'If any,' inserted Maggie.

'Don't be silly,' Tim chided, 'most certainly

tomorrow someone will be out after us. Two important people,' he laughed.

'But how will anyone know where to come?' Maggie feared.

'Jonas will exhaust every bolthole,' Tim replied.

'Bolthole?' She looked in the direction where Tim should be.

'Bolthole,' he repeated. 'Because you *were* intending to escape, weren't you, Maggie?'

Maggie dropped her head. 'Perhaps,' she told him, 'but I never let Jonas know.'

'There would be no need to, Jonas knows everything.'

'He couldn't!' she protested.

'No, he couldn't ... but he still does.' A pause. 'The thing is, I don't really know *what* my brother knows. I never did.' Before Maggie could break in, Tim resumed, 'One of those boltholes of yours would undoubtedly be the de Merrils, and Jonas would undoubtedly suspect that, and ring.'

'I expect so,' Maggie sighed. 'After all, he has rung there before.'

'You mean when you flew over with Helen to meet the de Merrils?'

'Yes, Jonas arranged it.' Maggie was silent for a moment. 'There doesn't appear to be as thick a curtain between Helen and Jonas as between Helen and you,' she said tentatively, hopeful for a response. When none came she pleaded: 'What is it, Tim? What is it all about? Can't I ever know?'

'You choose a wrong time to ask, Maggie,' Tim said ruefully. 'Here we are stuck in the desert and you land me with that!'

'Well, when is a right time, Tim? A right person? I've never really stopped asking since I came here: Grandfather and Helen and Jonas and you. But no result. Now I'm trying you again, wrong time though it may be. I want to be told the Renwick story, so make this the right time. Anyway, what else have we to do all night?'

Tim gave a dry cough. 'Am I that unattractive?' he asked.

'You're very attractive,' Maggie said, 'but what's that to do with it? Oh, I see what you mean.' She laughed without embarrassment. 'But it's not like that with us, is it?' she said frankly.

'Obviously, by your tone, it's not like that with you,' Tim replied humorously.

'And you?' Maggie included.

'Touché,' Tim retorted.

Although it was very dark now and she could not see him, she knew he was grinning. She did, too.

'Shake,' she invited, and their fingers sought entanglement, then stayed there.

Their hands were still enfolded when a sudden piercing light lit up their close proximity. On the blanketing sand, shod in silence, a four-wheel-drive had come right up. The first intimation they had of any arrival was an intense beam focussed ruthlessly on them. They sat blinking stupidly at it for a while, then scrambled to their feet. The driver, a black figure holding the powerful spotlight, had not said anything yet, but Maggie was sure that Tim knew, as she knew, that he would be Jonas.

Out of the darkness behind the blinding beam came four laconic words, and Maggie shrank from them.

'Am I spoiling something?' she heard.

Tim was walking into the light, shielding his eyes as he went. 'Thank heaven you came, Jonas, I wasn't fancying a night in this place.'

'It didn't look like it.' There was banter in Jonas's answer, but to Maggie's ears each word was a jeer.

'We'd just realised that darkness had caught us up,' Tim tried to explain. 'The engine spluttered out hours ago. We knew we could do nothing, so we stayed where we were—the old desert rule.' He said it confidently enough, but Maggie sensed he was not confident. She looked at him, then turned her glance to the face behind the glaring light.

'Commendable,' Jonas was drawling, 'but not so commendable not filling up before you left.'

'Yes, that was remiss of me,' Tim agreed. 'I was aware I would need more gas, then I forgot.'

'Well, don't forget again. Remember that our western tracks are greedy ones.'

'I will, Jonas,' Tim said, and Maggie felt sorry for him.

'I was in it, too,' she proffered. When Jonas ignored her she asked: 'How did you find out about us?'

Jonas answered with mock intrigue: 'What? Is there something to find out?'

'You know what I mean,' she snapped irritably.

'No, I don't know,' Jonas snapped back. 'Naturally I wondered when you were not in the office this morning. You see' ... a satisfied note ... 'I happened to pick on today to be there myself. I thought you might be ill, so I crossed to the homestead, only to be informed by Grandfather that you'd left early to put in a good day's work. Tell me, was it?'

'Was it what?' Maggie asked.

'A good day's work? A successful day's work? It certainly looked like it just now. It looked, too, as though you, and not Helen de Merril, came out the winner.'

'Really, Jonas——' Tim tried to break in.

'Shut up, Tim, you've caused me a damn lot of inconvenience, and the less I get from you the better. You should have conducted a tour this afternoon, did you know that?'

'Yes, but it was to be only a quick trip there and back, and I believed I'd be in time,' Tim appealed.

'Well, you weren't, so I cancelled the tour. Later on I had to come out to retrieve you.'

'How——' began Maggie again, but Jonas forestalled her.

'I rang the de Merrils, and fortunately Helen answered. She said you were both on the way home, and I was a little surprised. I'd only expected *one* return.' A look at Maggie. 'But no, Helen said both.'

Neither Tim nor Maggie commented, and Jonas went on.

'I did nothing then, believing you would make it before dusk. But at first dark I knew you couldn't, that you would have to stay out all night.'

'So you came for us?' Maggie said.

'I'm here, aren't I?'

'We would have been all right,' she mumbled.

'But very cold,' Jonas inserted drily. When Maggie did not speak, he drawled: 'I can assure

you that the desert gets *very* cold—even with close
settlement.' A pause. 'That, and the fact that even
in a place like Phineas Acres people can still talk,
brought me out here at once. I think' ... a hard
look at Maggie ... 'you should thank me, not
look disappointed.'

Maggie started to say something at that, then
decided to let it pass. Instead: 'Thank you,' she
shrugged—without thanks.

He waited a moment, his expression quizzical,
then he wheeled round and crossed to his vehicle,
climbed in, then reversed the waggon's direction
into a returning one. Maggie and Tim waited in
the darkness without a word.

When Jonas had his transport in the position he
required, he tossed out a towing rope to his
brother. 'I'm not just filling you up,' he indicated,
'I'm *taking* you. That's the only way to be sure
you'll get there.' There was deliberate disparage-
ment in his words.

'Make the tow-rope foolproof,' Jonas ordered,
'because if it snaps loose then you're on your own.
This is as far as I go with any help.'

But he did go a step further, he held the beam
aloft while Tim tied and fastened. When Tim had
finished, Jonas said shortly to Maggie: 'Hop in.'
She went to climb up beside Tim, but Jonas called
tersely: 'Not there, in the front vehicle.'

'Yours?'

'Yes.'

'I would sooner——' she began.

'So would I. But Tim will need all his attention
on the steering wheel, not on his passenger.'

'If you think——'

'I do think,' Jonas cut her short. 'Just get in.' He

turned back to Tim's jeep again.

'Take it easy,' he briefed. 'You'll be driving blind, so depend on me. Understand?'

'Yes, Jonas.'

'Is everything aboard? I don't want to come out again tomorrow for any left-behinds, tonight is more than enough.'

'Yes,' said Tim, 'everything is on. Actually, Jonas, we hadn't settled in for the night——' He stopped, a little uncomfortable.

Jonas did not notice his discomfort. He had his beam focussed on Tim's jeep, and he was looking hard at Maggie's small bag. He went across and picked it up, then strode to his own car where he threw the bag into the back seat.

'You'll need to travel as light as possible,' he said laconically to his brother, 'the sand can get tricky. Are you ready?'

'Ready, Jonas,' Tim replied.

'Then we're off.' Jonas jumped in his waggon and released the brake. He also extinguished his powerful torch, but the vehicle lights were even more powerful, and lit the way brilliantly. A very lovely way, had Maggie been in the mood to appreciate it, for the beam seemed to block out the ugliness, and the dry aridity became almost a fantasy place.

But she did not notice, her mind was on the bag he had thrown in. She knew he would say something about it.

Within minutes he did.

'So Tim was going, too,' he mused.

'It was *my* bag,' Maggie informed him.

'But big enough for two?' Jonas suggested. 'Room for basic requirements?'

'I beg your pardon?' she said frigidly.

'Oh, no, you don't,' Jonas came back at her, 'you hate me too much to beg.'

'Yes, I do dislike you,' she agreed.

'Dislike? That's a pale word.' Jonas repeated: 'Was he, Miss Wentworth? Was Tim going with you?'

'No, he was not, but he refused to let me cross to the de Merrils' alone, so he came too.'

'But you are still *here*.'

'What about it?' she queried crossly.

'Here! With a getaway bag!'

Maggie paused. 'Tim wasn't well,' she stated at last, 'I knew it was the wrong time to leave him.'

'That was your only reason?' Jonas asked tightly.

'Of course.'

'You just said it was the wrong time, does that mean you still intend to go?'

Again she said: 'Of course.'

'Then this might interest you.' Jonas slackened to indicate some track manoeuvre to the driver behind him.

'Yes?' Maggie asked indifferently ... but his reply cut through her indifference.

'You're not going,' he said calmly, resuming his driving.

'That's my prerogative to decide,' she flashed. 'You may be my employer, but you can't——'

'I can, and I will.'

'And can I ask how?' Maggie knew she should not have said that the moment she mouthed the words.

In the darkness he looked briefly at her; all she could see was a dark blur of face, but she could still see the brilliant cobalt eyes. They were riveting hers.

'Were Tim not behind us I would stop and show you,' he told her. 'Right now. As he is, it will wait.' He added: 'Take that as you want to, Maggie, as a promise or a threat.'

He drove on silently.

Through the dark nightscape they travelled. Maggie did not know how Jonas picked his way, for even though the light was powerful, the desert still lay like a solid black block, and occasionally the beam seemed incapable of penetrating it. But still he pushed on, at times leaning out to shout a warning to his brother of some hazard ahead. He must know this country like he knew himself, Maggie thought, and, impulsively, she said so aloud.

'I *am* this country,' he reminded her. 'Tim never was.'

Unexpectedly he turned to her once again. He asked: 'Could you be?'

'Could I be what?'

'This country, Maggie. Could you?'

Maggie started a cutting rejoinder. Be part of this savage land? Never. But halfway through, she found she could not finish it. She waited for a cutting rejoinder from him, probably deriding her dumbness, but none came. A silence settled between them, a peaceful kind of silence, for though they did not speak, Maggie, anyway, did not need to. She felt somehow that Jonas did not need to, either. She felt—she felt——

'The lights of home.' Jonas broke in on her thoughts, and she looked through the windscreen at the first shimmer from the caravans, the motel, the homestead. All at once she felt like crying out:

'Yes—*home*.'

Instead she said: 'If I hurry I could open up the store and be only a little late.'

'It's not opening tonight,' he answered, 'so there's no hurry. I put a notice on the window. No one will be hammering on the door.'

'Oh.' Maggie could not think of anything to add to that. Presently she said: 'Then I'll go over to Grandfather.'

'If it's for a meal, no hope. He's having a night off. Indeed, he's been invited out, first an address on Pioneer Phineas, then a camp barbecue. He's quite bucked. If you go over you'll find no one there.'

'I'm pleased for Grandfather, and I'll make a cup of tea and have an early night.'

'Just like that?' Jonas had pulled up now, and he turned to look at her. 'You put me to all this inconvenience, then prattle about a cup of tea and an early night!'

'Is there anything wrong with that?'

'There's everything damn well wrong, and you damn well know it! Oh, no, Miss Wentworth, you and I are going to have a few pertinent words.' He had said that before, Maggie remembered, and had them. Jonas and his pertinent words.

'Tim——' she mumbled.

'My words with Tim can wait till later. My words with you can't.'

He jumped out of the waggon and went back to his brother, now also alighting. Maggie heard him toss: 'I'll see you in the morning,' and heard Tim comply. Before she could make a move to escape, Jonas was back.

She went to get out to save him the trouble of issuing an order, but he surprised her by getting back into the driving seat, then leaning across her and locking the door.

Before she could comment he had sparked the engine again, accelerated, then swiftly he was leaving the garages behind them, the buildings. *The lights.*

In some dark paddock she knew she would never identify again, Jonas stopped. For a while he just sat there, arms folded, doing nothing, then he turned deliberately to her.

He kissed her.

In that single kiss Maggie knew a savagery she had never encountered before; she knew a lesson given and a lesson taken. Yet there was something else as well, and she could not turn away from it.

There was a deep intimacy there was no denying, not with his hands now on her breasts as he impelled her closer, not with his mouth seeking hers, not with that arrogant possession in his firming muscles. Most of all there was a *fusion*, even though there had been only one brief kiss, for in spite of that oneness, and nothing else with it, while the single kiss had lasted there had been unity.

'No!' Maggie protested, startled.

At once Jonas released her. In a more leisurely manner he took his pipe from his pocket. This time he actually lit up. She had never seen him smoke before, and she mumbled so.

'But you haven't really seen me before,' he

drawled in reply. 'You've looked the other way. You can look now.' His eyes challenged her. 'That's why I brought you out here.'

'You mean——' Maggie instinctively withdrew.

'No, I don't mean that, I mean just *look* at me sometimes, Maggie, *listen* when I speak to you. Surely you can do that?'

'But I don't like you.'

'I don't like you, but by heaven, I think I could love you.'

'Love me?' Now Maggie was stunned. 'Oh—you mean *that* love.'

'Love is what I said. Was my pronunciation wrong?'

'You mean love as—as——' Maggie stammered, and stopped.

'As the love act? Yes, I expect *you* would interpret it as that. *Brother Wolf.*' He showed his teeth in the darkness in a thin grin, and he looked, indeed, a wolf.

'I don't understand you,' she heard herself murmuring.

'But it seems by your interpretation of love you surely understand *this*.' The 'this' came indistinctly from between the cleavage of her bosom. His face was there, buried in the soft valley between her breasts. His hard skin grazed the softness, it hurt, but there was no withdrawal in Maggie. It was all she could do not to gather him closer, her heart was beating wildly, down there he *must* hear it and reach his interpretation.

With a supreme effort she pushed herself away from him and just as quickly he leaned over her as he had before, but this time to open the door.

'Find your own way home.' His voice was thick.

'It's dark—I can't see.'

'You'll be all right, you're a clever girl. Look what a fool you've made of me,' he said savagely.

'I've done nothing,' Maggie answered. 'You told me you would show me how you could stop me from leaving.'

'Did I? I must have been mad.'

'You no longer want to stop me?'

'Put it this way' . . . he was moving the waggon forward . . . 'that I'm no longer interested in the method. Not with you.'

He proceeded a few feet from where he had pushed her, then braked.

'Get in,' he called wearily. 'If I leave you, you might fall and break a leg.'

'That would worry you?' Maggie stumbled after the car and climbed up again. It was *very* dark and she did not look forward to walking.

'I would have to pay,' he reminded her shortly.

They did not speak a word to each other all the way back to the project. When they parted at the homestead they were still silent.

CHAPTER THIRTEEN

MAGGIE saw little of her boss in the following week. A fresh list of directions appeared on her desk each morning, and some time after she left at night Jonas must have checked her finished work, then left the completed pile for her filing or posting.

She encountered Jonas once outside the store, several times crossing to the homestead, but no words were exchanged, only cool nods.

Maggie was seeing little of Tim, too, and Grandfather, evidently sensing something amiss, was not his usual bright self. It began to jar on her, and, seeing she could not ignore Jonas's written orders, she felt sorely tempted to ignore his paying guests, except that that side of her work was the side she liked best. Also Tim, according to his brother, was being dilatory with the tours, so any discrepancy on her part might have made it worse for him. Maggie liked Tim too much for that ... but she still wished their guide would remember to appear when he should appear. Like this afternoon. Maggie decided to cross to Tim's section and give him a reminder.

She found Tim there, but not bent over a lump of rock as one might have expected. Instead he was staring out of the window. He turned as she entered.

'Maggie,' he said.

For some reason the obvious announcement irritated her. Liking Tim as she did, she wondered at herself when she snapped back: 'Who did you expect?'

Tim looked at her, a little boy lost look, and she regretted her abruptness. 'Everyone is touchy here,' she said lamely.

'The tourists?' Tim asked.

'Well, nothing's been dug up this week.' Maggie hunched her shoulders. 'However, they still seem to be enjoying themselves fairly well. Due' ... she tilted her chin ... 'solely to me. Neither you nor

Grandfather have been good company, and your brother never is. It's rather like an approaching storm.'

'I shouldn't think so,' Tim said factually, 'we never have rain.'

Maggie joined him at the window. 'Yet there must have been once,' she mused, 'because there was a river. Since then it's dried up, but when I went to the old mine——'

'Yes?' Tim's voice came a little angrily; he was always calm and slow-spoken, and she looked enquiringly at him.

He caught the look, and said: 'I had hoped you'd put that silly idea out of your head, Maggie.'

'What silly idea?'

'The mine. Your interest in the mine. Remember what happened before.'

'Yes—but before I got trapped in that sand, I stepped into a patch of mud.' A thought struck Maggie. 'But mud needs wet, yet you say——'

'Please, Maggie.' Tim came in quite shortly this time. 'Please don't cut a caper like that any more. The place is due for demolition. You could destroy yourself.'

'The way I feel now it wouldn't matter,' Maggie said gloomily, forgetting the mine. 'Everything seems brooding, somehow. You must feel it, Tim. I do.'

'You imagine things,' he answered. 'Also, if you came over here to remind me that I have a tour, I hadn't forgotten.'

He turned and left her rather rudely, something she had only known his brother do. Tim was always considerate, always polite.

She watched him climb the steps to the motel verandah to check his tour ladies. There was no spring about him, and Maggie felt in spite of his evasions that he was experiencing the same uncertainties and apprehensions as she was. But uncertain and apprehensive of what? She did not know, she was only aware of something about to happen, and it nagged at her.

But nothing did happen. One of the tourists eventually dug up some sapphire, which brought a new enthusiasm to the other diggers, so that helped.

It did not last long, though, and Maggie, lingering with the guests, gathered the fact that though they all had been interested and it was an experience they would not forget, they were still looking forward to bright lights again.

A point to Jonas? A point against Tim? Maggie grimaced. She wished it could be the other way. Yet looking at it with honesty instead of personal bias she sensed that Jonas was right, Tim wrong. Even with the ground at Phineas cracking everywhere ... except the old mine ... Maggie still felt Phineas was farming land, not gem terrain. Except the old mine. What had made her think of that again? She supposed it was because it was never far from her mind. In spite of her last disastrous exploration she knew she still wanted to return. But no, that was forbidden.

The days stumbled on, and Maggie's sense of uncertainty persisted. Then, on a particularly restless afternoon for her, Jonas still absent from the office, the phone rang. Maggie took it up. It was Helen.

Maggie had not been in touch with Helen since her journey back with Tim, that journey that had been supposed to provide her getaway from Phineas, but had finished up keeping her more hopeless a prisoner than ever.

For now, even though she believed that Jonas, following the paddock incident, would readily have rid himself of her, something else had happened. Happened this time to Maggie herself. Although she wanted no more of the place, although she hated the man who was king of the place, suddenly, unbelievably—but compulsively, *she wanted to stay*. She loathed her self-knowledge. She tried to disbelieve it. But the fact remained that she did not want to leave Phineas.

'Maggie!' Helen's voice came breathlessly through the wire. 'Maggie, you must be ready within the hour.'

'What?' Maggie managed to break in.

'For what you asked me, and what I agreed.'

'You mean——'

'Yes, Maggie. Everything's all right—everything is going to be fine. I know it will be.'

'What about your grandparents?'

'I said everything. Now hurry!'

'But in an hour——'

'No more. Wait on the strip, Maggie.' Helen's voice began to recede.

'With my bag?' Maggie inserted that before Helen could ring off.

There was a small silence at the other end, then a bright: 'Of course, Maggie.' The phone went down.

Maggie went to the door and looked out. Except

that she was at Phineas Acres where no rain fell she would have said a storm was rising. Suddenly she felt afraid.

She decided to ring Helen back, but at the last digit she put the phone down again. What can I say to Helen? she thought. Why am I hesitating to say it now? Why am I feeling like this?

At once a simple answer came to her. An answer so unwanted, so preposterous, so unthinkable, she would have nothing to do with it. But at least the basic realisation of it jerked her out of herself, so much so that she left the office immediately, crossed to the homestead and took up the bag she had never unpacked.

She did not seek out Grandfather, it was hard not to say goodbye, but it had to be like that. Hard, too, to ignore Tim—Maggie did not permit herself to think of Jonas.

Looking at her watch she knew it was time, and she set off. She was at the strip only minutes before the Cessna swooped over, Helen for some reason approaching lower than she ever had approached before.

Then Maggie saw that the approach was not the only thing that was different today. Helen was not controlling her craft as she always controlled it, in fact it appeared unsteady.

Maggie tossed her bag down . . . anywhere at all . . . she knew in a vague, yet somehow definite, way that she would not be needing the bag, that she would not be leaving. She began to run.

But though she started running first, a figure she had not noticed before outstripped her. The little plane was only several metres from the paddock now, but instead of landing it suddenly hiccoughed

upward again, then once more it descended, not to
rise this time. But there was still motion. The
Cessna began travelling drunkenly to the end of
the clearing. There was mulga and spinifex in its
path, a few tired gums. Beyond that a dip to the
dry river.

Maggie still ran, but blindly now. She wished
she could not hear as well . . . hear an impact.

In a moment she did. The plane hit the bushes,
but miraculously quite gently. Helen's small craft
shivered and sank down. It was all over.

It had barely finished when the runner in front
of Maggie had the Cessna door open, Helen in his
arms. Maggie watched as Jonas carried Helen
carefully away from the craft. At once she was
remembering another girl Jonas had carried . . .
but oh, how differently from *this*.

She ran over and knelt beside him.

'Is she——'

'She's all right,' Jonas judged. 'More than she
deserves for that fantastically bad piece of
airmanship. Or'—a pause—'*was it*?' Before
Maggie could question him, he said: 'Apart from
shock, I would predict only a few bruises.'

'And my ankle.' Helen, quite conscious, was
looking steadily up at Jonas, a very level, very
direct look. 'My ankle is broken.'

'I don't believe so,' Jonas said. Then, without
even looking at it, Maggie noted, he altered: 'Yes,
perhaps it is.' He was staring very levelly, very
directly back at Helen. After a lengthy pause he
turned to Maggie.

'All right, Miss Wentworth,' he ordered brus-
quely, 'get cracking. Do the usual things—prepare
a bed, fix hot water, hot tea with sugar, the rest of

the stunt. Haul out anything we might need from
the medical cabinet. After that get someone to
come out in a jeep to help me bring her
in.—And as you go——' A different note in his
voice now.

'Yes?' Maggie asked.

'Pick up that bag.' Without another word to
her, Jonas turned back to Helen.

In spite of the urgency of her orders, Maggie
still waited a moment to watch Helen and Jonas.

'So you did it,' Jonas was smiling at Helen. He
bent down and triumphantly kissed her. It was a
kiss like *she* had never had, Maggie knew.

'You should have done it years ago, Helen,'
Jonas continued, 'but at least you've done it now,
my girl.' With Maggie still watching, he kissed
Helen triumphantly again.

Maggie picked up her bag and walked back to
the project. She called in first at the bunkhouse
and instructed two of the men to hurry out to the
strip. She told them why.

'Was that the noise we heard?' They whistled.
'What will the boss need?'

'Transport back, your help with the patient, any
rugs and cushions you can find to soften the
journey.'

'Will do.' The men already were piling up a jeep,
starting the engine. As Maggie ran the rest of the
way to the homestead she heard them leave, and
she decided to enlist Grandfather's help to be
ready on time.

Between them they just made it as the jeep
pulled up at the bottom of the steps, the two men
in front, Helen supported by pillows and Jonas's
arms in the back. The three men made a stretcher

of their folded arms and Helen was carried inside, then lowered into her prepared bed. Maggie, who had found no time yet to select what might be needed from the medical cabinet, swooped on it and gathered a random armful. She went down the hall to the sickroom.

As she went, the two men were leaving. They nodded to Maggie . . . but one of them gave a grin and a wink. Maggie smiled back, a little nonplussed, but not when she reached the door. The door was shut—tightly.

She stood a moment, unsure of what to do. Because of her armful of bottles she could not turn the handle. How silly of Jonas to have closed the thing. She opened her mouth to ask to be let in, then remembered a grin and a wink. She felt her cheeks burning, and was glad of a few moments to let the heat fade out of them. Deciding to put her burdens on a nearby table, she turned, but low voices halted her. She could not decipher any words, but she could hear the deep intentness of them. She went down the hall and spent a while sorting out what she had grabbed up. She returned the superfluous medicines to the cabinet, then was able to carry the rest in one hand. The other hand, she thought, could open the door. *Knocking first.*

But when she returned, the door was open again. Helen was well propped up by pillows, and she appeared very comfortable and not at all in pain. Also more beautiful than frightened.

'Am I?' Helen smiled of the latter when Maggie said it. 'Yet I *was* frightened, Maggie. However, apart from my ankle my doctor' . . . Helen looked

up at Jonas . . . 'feels certain I'm quite sound.' She
gave a low laugh. 'He's put the tape measure over
me.'

. . . Yes, Brother Wolf would. That came
unbidden to Maggie's mind and nearly to her lips.
She heard herself rushing in with something about
ringing the flying doctor.

'The F.D. won't be needed,' Jonas said crisply.
'I've a pretty good know-how in this sort of thing.
Out here it's necessary. Now let's see what you've
chosen to mend the patient, nurse. Yes, it seems
satisfactory. You could be something of a medico
yourself.'

'Out on the Reef,' Maggie provided in her turn,
'I had to have some knowledge, too. I've brought
strapping, liniment, painkillers, and, of course, the
hot tea.' She turned and took the tea from
Grandfather, who had come to the door. She
passed the cup to Helen.

While Helen sipped the sweet brew, Maggie and
Jonas bathed, anointed and strapped the foot, then
Maggie arranged a supportive pillow under it, a
light rug on top for warmth.

Jonas meanwhile was watching their casualty.
He turned to Maggie. 'I'd change that painkiller to
a sleep-inducer,' he said in a voice for her alone.
He indicated Helen's drooping eyelids. 'She's more
exhausted, I would say, than pained. Up, no
doubt,' he added, 'with the birds.' He looked
narrowly at Maggie. 'Were *you*?'

'If you mean by the birds was I up early, why
should I have been?' she retorted.

'With accompanying bag?' he asked.

'Which I decided wasn't needed,' Maggie said
levelly.

One of his brows shot up at her. 'And when did that decision occur?'

'Actually before Helen crashed,' she returned.

'Handy to recall that *now*,' Jonas shrugged, 'now that Helen no longer can take you out of Phineas.'

'Then can I leave with the outgoing tourists?' Maggie burst in quite desperately. She knew in that moment that she had to be finally rid of the place, finally rid of him. It had to be soon . . . *now*. That thought was uppermost.

Jonas did not answer her for almost a minute, in fact his attention seemed only on Helen, who was nearly asleep by this. He got up and took the emptied cup from her limp hand and passed it to Maggie. As he did so he mused: 'So more changes are in the wind.'

'Changes?' Maggie asked stupidly.

'Changes of mind. *Your* mind. Just now you discarded a getaway bag as no longer needed, but now it appears it is needed, in other words once more you want out. It's all rather pathetic.'

'Nonetheless it's so,' Maggie said. Seeing Helen's head droop, she leaned over and slipped one of the pillows away from her, then settled her back in the bed. After that she enquired crisply: 'What are my orders, Doctor?'

'As well as the requirements you already know I'd damn well like to be kept up to date with your latest whims, Nurse,' he came back.

'I've told you,' Maggie answered. 'I'm leaving here.'

'If only I could be certain of that,' he said angrily, and before she could reply he turned and went.

She drew up a chair and sat watching Helen in case there was some reaction. She did not think there would be, she had too much respect for Jonas Renwick's judgement, but if a delayed concussion did set in, at least she would be on hand.

She remained there the rest of the day. Grandfather brought in a meal and she ate it, still watching Helen. He came in with tea and found her still there.

Around dusk Helen awoke, refreshed, quite hungry, but, or so she said after some quick consideration, still sore.

'Of course,' Maggie soothed, 'yet the ankle isn't swollen.'

'It hurts,' insisted Helen. She glanced to the window. 'Night already. When do you go to the store, Maggie?'

'The usual time. But of course I won't go tonight.'

'Because of me? But that's silly. I'm perfectly all right ... I really mean I'm not seriously ill, anything like that. I could just rest here while you go. And *shouldn't* you go, Maggie?'

Maggie admitted she should, but she added that Brother Wolf probably would waive tonight's attendance.

'Brother Wolf,' smiled Helen fondly.

A little irritated, Maggie said: 'Well, isn't he, compared to Tim?'

'I don't know about Tim,' Helen said flatly. At once she asked: 'Could I use the phone and ring up Baden Wald, do you think?'

'Ring your grandparents,' said Maggie, 'but I thought they had left.'

'I never said so,' Helen reminded her, 'I just told you that everything would be all right.'

'And now it isn't? Will you tell them that?'

'I'll tell them where I am,' was all Helen's reply.

'In bed at Phineas with a damaged ankle? Won't that worry them?'

'Not,' said Helen, 'when I say I'm *here*.' A pause. 'Oh, Maggie, don't let's play about any more. You must know how wonderful this is for me. You must know why.'

'Because of something you once said,' Maggie nodded. 'Yes, Helen, I know.'

'Then help me, Maggie,' Helen begged.

Maggie caught the appeal in her voice and looked at her.

'Open the store tonight,' Helen pleaded. 'Leave me by myself.'

'Leave you *both*, you mean,' Maggie said intuitively.

'Oh, Maggie, you do understand!'

'Yes, Helen, I do.' But Maggie said it wearily, all at once she felt drained.

But in spite of her weariness, at opening time she crossed to the store, and it proved a busy hour. The present group were approaching the end of their tour, and were eager to stock up with souvenirs. The gem section was the most popular. Not many stones had been prospected, so, determined to prove they had been fossicking, the anxious customers were turning over the rock specimens, some confiding to Maggie that they intended to show the stones back home as their own finds. Others, won by finished presentations, bought the gems packed in velvet boxes. Meanwhile the usual sales went on, the everyday things that people must have, and Maggie would have welcomed help. Of late Tim had come to lend a hand, on several occasions Jonas had strolled in. But tonight she had to cope alone.

At last the hour was up, and she was closing the door, switching off the light.

She locked up, then went exhaustedly in the direction of the homestead. It had been a long, trying day. If Maggie had been honest she would have tacked on 'emotionally trying' as well. But she put any such thought aside.

She stumbled on, literally stumbled, for once more she had forgotten a torch. Never mind, Grandfather would have the homestead bright with lights.

Why am I so tired, she asked herself as she went, why am I so unhappy? Then she was remembering that simple, unwanted, preposterous answer she had reached the last time she had asked herself this: it had been the basic realisation that she loved the man she believed she hated. She cared for Jonas. For Brother Wolf.

At that moment she looked towards the homestead. A light was on in the room that had been allotted to Helen. It was a dimmed light for the patient's comfort, but it still lit up two figures.

One was Helen. She must have got up from her bed, because Maggie could see the fan of the dressing gown she had loaned her, though she could not see her face.

Neither could she see the face of the man with his back to the window *but his arms around Helen*.

With a sob she could not control Maggie stumbled the rest of the way home.

CHAPTER FOURTEEN

WHEN had she come to care for Jonas Renwick? When had it begun to matter that some other woman was in his arms?

Maggie could not have answered either question, but she was sharply aware that at no time had the man not strongly affected her, stirred her as she never had been stirred by any other male.

She had always been physically alerted by Jonas, but, despising herself for it, she had concealed it. Yet unsuccessfully, it seemed, for in spite of all her pushing aside, that feeling still was there. That vibrant consciousness.

But with it now had come love. Not the trappings of love, but the core. This, Maggie found, could not be pushed aside. With shame she faced up to the fact that she loved a man who loved someone else. But she could do nothing about it.

Everything was neatly packaged, Maggie thought, and if she had any doubt about that she needed only to look up at that window again . . . which she wouldn't. Finally, she did, though, but the silhouette was over, no figures were on display.

She climbed the last homestead step. As she had expected there was only Helen now in the allotted bedroom. For a yearning moment she tried to believe she had only dreamed that tender scene. But she hadn't. It had happened, and Maggie now called on all her resources to see the act through.

She smiled brightly at Helen.

Helen smiled brightly back. She looked tired but happy. She asked: 'Busy hour?'

'Very,' nodded Maggie. 'The present tourists are ending their stint quite soon, so they're buying up the souvenirs.' She sat down on the bed near Helen. She waited a moment, then asked deliberately: 'When do we move out?' It was mean of her, but she considered she deserved some kind of subtitle under that romantic scene just now.

'Move out, Maggie?' Helen looked puzzled.

'You and I were escaping, remember?'

'Of course.' Helen pleated the top of the sheet. 'Unfortunately,' she said, 'I don't know about my physical condition yet.'

'You look fine, Helen,' Maggie praised, 'indeed as good as I've ever seen you.'

'Perhaps, but could I fly as far as The Alice with an injured foot?' Helen gave her a worried look.

'You're right, of course,' Maggie conceded, 'and that is why tomorrow I *will* ring the Flying Doctor.'

'But Jonas said——'

Maggie got abruptly up from the bed and went to the window, the window where only a short time ago she had seen a man's strong arms entwining a girl. Jonas's arms. Damn Jonas, she was thinking, if he really cares for this girl he's made her wait a long, long time for his caring, then if he doesn't care he's only playing with her as he played with me, so he's *very much* Brother Wolf.

'Brother Wolf,' picked up Helen, and Maggie

realised she had spoken the name aloud. 'That's not nice of you, Maggie—Jonas is everything good, everything fine.'

'If you want it like that,' Maggie shrugged. She asked carelessly: 'What about Brother Lamb?' At Helen's enquiring look she said: 'Tim.'

'Tim.' Helen barely mouthed the name. She gave Maggie a quick glance, so swift Maggie could not have said what it held.

A moment went by in silence, then Maggie, having nothing more to say, insisted that she tuck Helen in, fetch some warm milk.

Helen did not protest, but almost before Maggie reached the door she was drifting off. Maggie decided to leave the milk and to go to bed herself.

Helen remained an invalid for the next few days, and everyone seemed contented that she do so.

When Maggie relayed the news to her that the engineering shop had overhauled her little Cessna and pronounced it now airworthy, Helen only smiled and thanked her for the message.

'When——' Maggie began once more, but this time Helen looked reproachful.

'Maggie, it wasn't fun making an emergency landing.'

Maggie restrained herself from asking, 'Even after practising it like you did?' and said instead, 'You have no after-effects, though, do you?'

'Who knows exactly what one has?' shrugged Helen. 'Things can come later. Also, Maggie, this ankle has to be perfect before we take off.'

'We? Then we're really going at last?'

'Dear Maggie, just be patient.' Helen put out her hand, a slender white hand and yet so capable, Maggie knew. She looked down at the girl, lovelier somehow than she had ever been, and she softened.

'I think you're a fraud,' she admitted, 'but a beautiful fraud. I don't understand you, Helen, I don't understand any of this, but——' She smiled, and took the hand.

When Helen reached the stage of getting up and limping to the window, Maggie had more time to herself. Although twice daily she still opened the store, although each morning she reported to the office, Jonas never made contact with her, neither to ask how business was, nor to leave work on her desk. It was as though although she was there she was not there. At times Maggie even believed it herself.

Because of her idle hours, one afternoon she crossed to the old mine. As she went slowly over she knew that her return to the mine was inevitable. Not since she first had come to Phineas had she completely put the place out of her mind. She knew when she left the Acres, as she must leave some time, she would always recall the derelict rig with the same curiosity and hope ... hope? ... that she did now. She also knew that she had to get inside again, more carefully this time, find out why she had been so oddly attracted before.

There was no one to watch her. The tourists were out on their final prospecting, Jonas was on one of his eternal missions, Grandfather doing his usual chores, Helen still in bed or sitting by the window, Tim, she presumed, still staring as he always did into space. In every way it was a good time to go.

When she reached the ruin she circled it cautiously. She neither wanted to drown in sand, nor be hauled up and bawled out by an angry man. Though *would* Jonas bawl her out again, would he be interested enough, now that he had agreed that she should go? 'If only I could be certain of that,' he had said.

Maggie decided at last on the back door to the mine; it was shut, but obviously it would be easy entry, to judge by its rusted bolts and handle. She pushed and found it responding at once. This time she had brought her torch and she shone it ahead. She probed first with a stout stick she had also brought, finding to her relief no soft earth to trap her. She started off.

The ground remained hard and flinty, no danger of smothering here. Carefully, step by step, Maggie proceeded, noting that she was descending gradually but progressively, and, since she had been on the track for more than five minutes, that she must have gone a fair way down.

Some time later she heard a noise and stopped to listen. It was not in here, it was outside, and it sounded very much like the engine of a plane. She listened more intently, then recognised that throb. The charter was more vibrant, as to be expected from a larger craft, this beat was minor. It was, it had to be, unless someone else had an identical Cessna, Helen's little machine.

But Helen was in bed ... or sitting at a window

and waiting for—— Maggie turned her thoughts away from that.

It was then she heard the other noise, but this time within the mine. She shone the torch and at first saw nothing. Then she focussed on the squelchy rocks, the shining wet ground, a dampness everywhere, understandable when at the base of everything flowed a narrow but steadily flowing stream.

A stream here! In dry, scorched, arid, cracking Phineas Acres! Where did it come from? Where did it go?

At that moment Maggie saw that someone stood by the stream, and she slowly raised the torch from the feet of the person on the edge of the water to the face.

Jonas Renwick's face. Jonas Renwick's eyes, even brilliant cobalt in this poor light, watching her. For some reason she could not have given Maggie extinguished her light, for she knew it would make no difference. No difference to Jonas, none to her. He would still cross to her, and she would still be waiting. She shivered almost ecstatically as she did.

But when Jonas reached her side, he extinguished his torch, too, to preserve its power. They stood, but apart, in the complete dark.

After a while Maggie knew she must say something. She listened to the soft flow of the stream and asked: 'Did you know there was water?'

'Always.'

'How long has it been here?'

'Ever since the river went underground some generations ago.'

'You didn't give me any such impression when you rescued me,' Maggie accused.

'The time wasn't ready,' he replied.

'Did Tim know?'

'Of course.'

'Then why——'

'Why didn't I say so when I so desperately needed water to make this country again what it was intended to be? I did it for Tim.'

'But you just said that Tim knew.'

'But thought I didn't. He kept the "knowledge" to himself.'

'Because he wanted rocks, not sheep?'

'No, you little fool, because he wanted Helen.'

'Helen?' Maggie stared through the darkness where Jonas must stand.

'Yes, I said Helen,' Jonas repeated.

'But Helen wanted—she wanted——'

'She wanted Tim in her turn. She always did want him. They wanted each other from the first day they met, and that's a long time ago. They say love can't start so young, but, heaven knows, it did for those two.'

'I don't understand,' puzzled Maggie.

'And I don't intend to tell you down here, Maggie. I'm not a mine man, I'm a plainsman. For the love of sky and grass, even meagre grass, let's get out of here.' Jonas put out a hand, and the touch of it electrified Maggie.

But it was only a hand as far as Jonas was concerned. Just a guiding touch. Jonas led Maggie up, then out. Once there they crossed to the sparse shade of a tree again, and he began once more.

'Tim never came over here—that is, not
noticeably. He must have come, of course,
otherwise he wouldn't have known about the
source, not have guarded the "secret" so jealously.
And why, you ask? Tim guarded it because he
believed if I knew I would cancel his gem
nonsense, blow this place up, release the stream to
start the Reptile River again. Begin once more
from where nature left off.'

'Would you have done that?' Maggie asked.

'Not then. Not with Tim as he was. But now, of
course, I will.'

'But your brother——'

'My brother Timothy will be well away from it
all. In fact he's gone now—in a small Cessna,
piloted by Helen.'

'By *Helen*? You knew this all the time?'

Jonas laughed. 'I had a pretty good idea.'

'But—but Helen wanted you!' Maggie burst
out.

In the dazzling sunshine, dazzling after the
gloom of the mine, Jonas stared at her a long
time.

'Oh, come off it,' he said at last.

'But it's true. And you wanted her. You said it
was important.'

'I said important *for us*.' Jonas looked deeply at
her.

Maggie stammered: 'I saw you in a window.'

'I saw some things in a window, too,' Jonas
reminded her tersely. He waited a moment. 'No,
never Helen, Maggie, not for me, only Helen for
Timothy. Right from childhood it was Helen and
Tim. Only' . . . a twist to his mouth . . . 'something
came between them.'

'It was the accident, wasn't it?' Maggie said intuitively.

'The one that took four lives and two hearts,' Jonas nodded.

'I still don't understand.'

'I know, and this time you're going to be told. It's an unbelievable story, but believe it.'

'Yes?' waited Maggie.

Jonas took his pipe out of his pocket, fingered it, replaced it.

'Tim kept the fact of the stream to himself because he felt it was his assurance some day of winning Helen. He didn't know how, but he stayed doggedly on, pursuing some role or other, anything to keep him here—tour captain, gem mentor.' Jonas shrugged. 'He was neither, nor was he a sheep man, even an outdoors man. He was just Tim. A spatter of knowledge, a grain of interest, but that was all. His only real interest was, and always has been, Helen.'

'Then why didn't they come together before?' Maggie asked.

'Good question, but not so good to answer. You see, it wasn't easy for that unhappy pair to live out life like life was doled out to them.'

'What do you mean, Jonas?'

'I mean' . . . a pause . . . 'that between them they killed four people. Of course it wasn't like that at all. Also it wasn't our father, either. It was simply, tragically, as the police maintained, a bad stretch of road, a bad night, a stone, a stump, something, anything, who knows? But that something—anything—took four lives.'

Maggie added: 'And two hearts. But *how*?'

'It's not a pleasant story, Maggie.' Jonas

sighed. 'You see, Helen's father and our mother were——' His voice broke off. He was silent for a long while, and Maggie did not break in. Presently he continued, but still leaving a gap.

'I don't believe either Uncle Maxim ... Tim and I called him that ... nor Linda, our mother, started off intending anything, but the fact remains it finally came to that.'

'To an attachment?' Maggie asked.

'To the beginnings ... perhaps more ... of an affair.'

'And your father, was he attracted to Helen's mother?' Maggie asked next.

'Was it a foursome, you mean? Not as far as we knew.'

'You're telling me that you three children understood what was taking place?'

'Oh, yes' ... grimly ... 'we understood. I at seventeen naturally would have, but I expect that pair at barely thirteen more or less stumbled on it. God knows it was obvious enough.'

'And it affected them?' Maggie said quietly.

'You've seen how it's affected them,' Jonas replied. 'It meant ten years of nothing at all for two hurt, lost, bewildered kids.'

'Yet it never affected you, Jonas.'

'Oh, yes, it did. It made me hard ... bitter.'

'A woman-hater,' Maggie came in.

'Yes. Until——'

She looked enquiringly at him, but he did not finish. Instead he resumed the story.

'No, it was never a foursome, Maggie. As far as I know Helen's mother and our father never retaliated, never played tit for tat. So' ... a tight smile ... 'it was never like father like son, was it? for he, as far as I knew, was never Father Wolf.'

'I should never have called you that,' Maggie murmured.

'No?' The brows above the cobalt eyes lifted. 'But I do believe I gave you some cause.'

'Go on,' urged Maggie of the story.

'I don't know at what period we young ones actually knew, but I do know it was catastrophic for Tim and Helen. They never said anything, but, as I was their fairly near contemporary, and always close to them, their shock was very clear to me. They were barely adolescent, vulnerable— remember, I was past all that. Anyway, Helen was a girl, and Tim—well, he was more finely-honed than I. To put it briefly, he and Helen saw what was happening—and flinched. Flinched, Maggie, is my word.'

'But what *happened*, Jonas?' Maggie insisted.

'An accident did. I was asleep that night of the disaster, or so, for everyone's sake, I told the police.'

'For everyone's sake?' She stared at him.

'Yes,' Jonas said. 'As you're aware, because Grandfather would have told you, our father was driving. Whether that was because he knew the road better than Maxim or because Maxim wanted a back seat with our mother' . . . a harsh note now in Jonas's voice . . . 'I'll never know. But I do know, Maggie, because I was *not* asleep, that my father was driving as he always drove, and that was responsibly. But the two young ones did not know. They'd absorbed the seat arrangement for the long journey—Helen's mother beside our father, the three children in a row behind the front driving seat, Maxim and Linda at the back, and when Father swerved as he did they thought in their disturbed minds that it was only because of that.'

'You mean they actually believed your father was so distressed he wanted to——'

'To finish everything and everybody? Yes. It was their age, Maggie, their sensitive make-up. Who knows what kids in puberty go through?'

'But you didn't,' Maggie reminded him again.

'I was older,' Jonas shrugged.

'I don't think you would have, anyway.'

'You really mean I'm too tough, too rough, too——' Jonas grinned all the way now.

'Finish the story,' Maggie prompted.

'When Father swerved across the track four young hands interfered. The first two were Helen's. Instinctively she leaned over to right the wheel. At once Tim leaned over to correct what she had done.'

There was a long pause now.

'Yes, Jonas?' Maggie whispered.

'Between them, or so they believed, and have believed since, they plunged the car off the road.' Another pause. 'And four people were killed.'

'But surely you could have spoken up, Jonas,' Maggie protested, 'prevented all these years of trauma.'

'If I had spoken,' Jonas said carefully, 'I would have had to include the two young ones, which would have been disastrous for them.'

'But hasn't it been a disaster as it is?'

'A lesser one,' he dismissed. 'As it was, at no

time was *anyone* blamed. The police were absolutely satisfied it was the condition of the road and a bad night. Who was I to include four interfering hands?'

'What happened then?'

'Everything,' Jonas said wearily. 'Helen had a very long, very distressing breakdown, Tim was little better. Both of them had to be kept at home.'

'And they never met,' provided Maggie.

'No. That was bad. But my grandfather had all he could cope with, and Helen's people had very little English in the beginning. Also the two families were a hundred miles apart.

'Then when Helen grew up her grandparents realised the few years they had left, and they became anxious for their granddaughter. There was no one else out here, and any-way——'

'Anyway, why shouldn't a Renwick pay a debt?' came in Maggie. She said in a low voice: 'And I believed the payment was you, Jonas.'

There was a long silence, then Jonas said: 'You mad, mad girl!'

'How was I to know? Helen came to the doorway at Baden Wald and said "I love him".'

'And immediately you—— Yes, a mad, mad girl.'

'Also you took Helen in your arms when she crashed,' Maggie said.

'A well-rehearsed crash,' Jonas admired. He asked: 'What other way did you want me to remove her? Drag her by her feet?'

'You carried her gently. You kissed her.'

'Did you want me to attack her instead?'

'Of course not, but it was a triumphant kiss.'

'I was triumphant. At last Helen had *acted*, something I'd tried for from Tim for years, but Tim was not as strong as Helen. He never will be. But they'll get through.'

'Still with that cloud over them?' doubted Maggie.

'Helen's cloud passed over when she first began flying in here, but the awkwardness, the silence of ten years was too much. You helped there.'

'I could have helped more had I known,' Maggie complained. 'Why wasn't I told, Jonas?'

'Because,' Jonas said simply, 'when you really look at it all, bring it down to basics, it still comes back to that old girl meets boy, girl parts from boy, girl and boy come together again. Doesn't it?'

'Perhaps,' admitted Maggie. 'But will they stop like that? Will they still be together?'

'That pair were designed in heaven,' said Jonas with feeling. A pause. 'Not like two others I know.'

Without warning he leaned over and pulled her to him, and his touch aroused every sensual sensation she had in her, and much more than that it filled her heart. His cobalt eyes possessed her, but she stopped gladly in his possession, aware she would never be free again, never alone, yet bowing eagerly to such a fate.

He must have felt here complete submission, for he said with sudden strength: 'My God, I promise you that you will feel loved when I do love you, Maggie.'

Maggie heard herself asking: 'When will that be?'

'After, not before,' he rationed blandly, 'Grandfather would want it like that.'

'And you? What would you want?' dared Maggie.

'What do you think?' he replied angrily, then the anger left him and he put out a finger and began moving it experimentally over Maggie's lower lip.

'If Helen and Tim were designed in heaven,' Maggie asked, tantalised beyond belief by that finger travelling tenderly on her lip, 'where were that other pair you know designed?'

'In a den,' Jonas said readily. 'Don't forget I'm Brother Wolf.' The finger was leaving her lip now, Jonas's mouth taking its place. He pressed down a first, a second kiss ... *more* ... but Maggie still knew that each kiss would always be new and beautiful to her, and she smiled.

'What are you grinning at, Miss Wentworth?' Jonas demanded, and Maggie in her turn ran her finger along his lip. When her mouth took over, as his had, Jonas could barely hear Maggie's answer to his question.

But he did hear: 'I'm smiling at *Brother* Wolf changing to *Lover* Wolf, Mr Renwick.'

He did not keep Maggie waiting for her proof.

Harlequin® Plus

BIRTHSTONES

GARNET (January)—a semi-precious deep red stone said to have the power to protect travelers.

AMETHYST (February) — pale lavender to deep purple gems once worn to cure drunkenness.

AQUAMARINE (March)—a blue - green symbol of the sea believed to cure laziness.

DIAMOND (April) — a symbol of love prized for jewelry; also the hardest known natural substance.

EMERALD (May)—a favorite gem of Cleopatra's, its green depths thought to be good for the eyes.

PEARL (June) — a lustrous product of the oyster believed to have the power to lengthen life.

RUBY (July) — a blood-red precious jewel valued not only for ornamentation but also for precision instruments.

PERIDOT (August)—an emblem of serenity ranging in color from yellow-green to deep olive.

SAPPHIRE (September) — a cornflower-blue jewel once considered a charm against evil.

OPAL (October) — an iridescent stone that should be worn only by people born in October; bad luck for others.

TOPAZ (November)—a glowing yellow gem long ago believed to bring friendship to its wearer.

TURQUOISE (December)—a bright sea-blue opaque stone that should be given, never bought.

Great old favorites...
Harlequin Classic Library

The **HARLEQUIN CLASSIC LIBRARY** is offering some of the best in romance fiction— great old classics from our early publishing lists.

Complete and mail this coupon today!

Harlequin Reader Service

In U.S.A. 2504 W. Southern Avenue
Tempe, AZ 85282

In Canada 649 Ontario Street
Stratford, Ontario N5A 6W2

Please send me the following novels from the Harlequin Classic Library. I am enclosing my check or money order for $1.50 for each novel ordered, plus 75¢ to cover postage and handling. If I order all nine titles at one time, I will receive a FREE book, *Hospital Nurse*, by Lucy Agnes Hancock.

☐ 127 **For Ever and Ever**
    Mary Burchell

☐ 128 **Dear Intruder**
    Jane Arbor

☐ 129 **Who Loves Believes**
    Elizabeth Hoy

☐ 130 **Barbary Moon**
    Kathryn Blair

☐ 131 **Magic Symphony**
    Eleanor Farnes

☐ 132 **Mountain of Dreams**
    Barbara Rowan

☐ 133 **Islands of Summer**
    Anne Weale

☐ 134 **Night of the Hurricane**
    Andrea Blake

☐ 135 **Young Bar**
    Jane Fraser

Number of novels checked @ $1.50 each =	$ _____
N.Y. and Ariz. residents add appropriate sales tax	$ _____
Postage and handling	$ ___.75
	TOTAL $ _____

I enclose _____
(Please send check or money order. We cannot be responsible for cash sent through the mail.)

Prices subject to change without notice.

Name _____
(Please Print)

Address _____
(Apt. no.)

City _____

State/Prov. _____ Zip/Postal Code _____

Offer expires August 31, 1984   40256000000